Misguided Target

Misguided Target

Jessica Page

Third Edition
Published 2016 by Creativia
Book design by Creativia (www.creativia.org)
Cover art by "Book Cover by Design"
This book is a work of fiction. Names, characters, places, and incidents are the product of the author's imagination or are used fictitiously. Any resemblance to actual events, locales, or persons, living or dead, is purely coincidental.

Dedication

To my mother,

A strong, beautiful and intelligent woman who raised me to understand that life is made up of choices with consequences — some good and some bad — but in the end they all help shape who we are.

"Always be kind, for everyone is fighting a hard battle."—— Plato

Chapter 1

Kendall

Not in my wildest dreams could I have predicted this is where my life would be today. Most people don't wake up one morning and say, "I want to be an escort," but that's exactly what I did. Don't get me wrong, it's not exactly a dream job, but working at some box store for minimum wage wouldn't be either. That's likely what would have happened, if I'd stayed in the small town where I grew up in Minnesota. I'd probably still be living in some rundown house, married to a man I hated, with at least two kids by now. That might work for some people, but not me. It may be harshly stereotypical for a girl raised by an alcoholic mother with an absentee, jailbird father, but it doesn't change the fact that it's the sad reality for many others like me. That's the life I was born into – it would likely have been the life I died in – if I hadn't made the choice to do something about it. I would say that things are better now, but life has quite the sense of humor, and it took me becoming an escort to have the chance at this better existence. That's not exactly something you'd print on a high school guidance brochure. But when opportunity knocked on my door I took it – right or wrong – and I've never looked back.

It all started about seven years ago, just after my high school graduation. I was eighteen and I'd finally had enough of my mom's creep, loser boyfriend venturing into my room late at night. Most of the time, he just stood in the doorway, staring at me creepily as he mumbled things about how 'tight my body was' and wondering 'what I tasted like', but that night was different. I remember being woken up to the sound of the cheap floors creaking beneath his weight as he approached my bed. I felt suddenly sickened by the overpowering smell of tobacco on his clothes and his breath as he leaned in to smell my hair.

"God you smell so good," he purred in his raspy voice.

"Get the hell out of here!" I demanded before he placed his filthy, nicotine-stained hand over my mouth. The look in his eyes told me he wasn't going to stop this time. I bit his hand as hard as I could and kneed him in the chest, causing him to stumble back a little. I didn't have time to defend myself from the hard slap he sent across my face. I remained a little disoriented as I felt him climb back on top of me. When he greedily reached for my pajama bottoms, I seized my opportunity and grabbed for the lamp on the bedside table. I remember smashing it as hard as I could over his head, knocking him unconscious.

"What did you do to him?" my mother cried, stumbling into the room and ignoring the broken pieces of porcelain on the ground as she bent to tend to him.

"Are you serious? Isn't it obvious?" I'd asked, dumbfounded that she hadn't figured it out. "Your fucking creep of a boyfriend just tried to rape me!"

"You little slut liar!" she screamed, wiping blood off his head with her tattered gray housecoat. "He would never do that to me! He loves me."

I stared at her in disbelief for what felt like a very long time. I knew my mother was a pathetic individual, but a woman who would pick this sad, sleazy excuse for a human being over her daughter didn't deserve to have one.

I'd had enough of this house and this life. If she was happy living like this I couldn't stop her, but I wasn't going to. Not anymore. A part of me was sad I hadn't killed him, as I listened to him telling her ridiculous things about how he was sleepwalking and that I'd attacked him wanting sex, even though he tried to fight me off. I quickly packed up a bag of belongings, along with the few hundred dollars I'd managed to save from working at the local diner, and I got the hell out of there, moving to downtown Minneapolis to start fresh.

It was terrifying to be in the big city alone. I mean, living with my mother hadn't been a glamorous life, but at the very least I never had to worry about a roof over my head and food in my belly. At first, I found a cheap motel to stay at and to say that it was awful would be a slight understatement. I had my high school diploma, but that wasn't exactly a gateway to good employment. The little money I had didn't last long and for a while, I even considered going back. But I decided to quit the 'pity party' I'd been throwing myself and managed to get a job doing something I was familiar with – waitressing at a twenty-four-hour diner. It wasn't a fancy place, but it was clean, and it put some much-needed money in my pocket.

After about a month, a man came in during one of my midnight shifts, joined by a few of his friends. I learned that he owned a high-end bar downtown and that the others with him were members of his staff. They flirted harmlessly and were easy to get along with. Apparently they liked to gorge on greasy food after a busy night. To this day I still don't know why he offered me a job in his bar. I don't know if he actually thought I was a good waitress, or just felt bad for me because I was young and cute and stuck in a dump like this. Whatever his reasons were I lucked out, and he offered me a good job. It was a place that was rather selective about their clientele. Then again, an establishment that charged as much as they did for drinks would only be appealing to certain individuals. It was the kind of place where customers paid handsomely to be served and liked their service to include a side order of cleavage and shameless flirting, to boost their already inflated egos. I was good at that job. I was pretty enough to get people's attention and smart enough to keep it. I'm not the most beautiful woman in the world – far from it – but bronzed skin, long black hair, gray eyes and high cheekbones are a conversation starter, and after that my well-proportioned breasts did most of the talking. It's funny, because I've had people tell me it's conceited or arrogant to use beauty to get ahead, but the sad truth is you need to make the most of what you're given in this life. I didn't have the luxury of not using everything I could.

About eight months into my employment at the downtown bar, I was starting to experience a little stability in my life. I had an apartment with a roommate; a few friends and I was starting to feel somewhat content. Little did I know that everything was about to change – that's when I met Senator James Clarke.

Although he wasn't a stranger to politics, at the time he was a newly-elected senator. I remember being mesmerized by this gorgeous man in his early forties, wearing a suit that probably cost more than everything I owned, combined. He wasn't exactly a regular, but he did come in from time to time when his employment brought him back to his home state. He was always charming and a pro at innocent flirting, but he never paid me much attention – until one fateful day. I remember it was busy that evening, and I couldn't help noticing how handsome he was as he sat down alone in my section. It was the first time I'd had the opportunity to serve him.

"Can I get you a drink?" I asked him with my most flirtatious smile.

"Bourbon on the rocks and whatever you're having, Kendall," he offered casually, casting me a sexy smirk as he read my nametag.

"I can't, I'm working. Besides, I'm not twenty-one, so the boss has me under strict orders to behave," I replied innocently, still flirting with him.

"When do you get off?"

"Twenty minutes."

"Well then, I'd like to get that bourbon now and then, once you're off work, you can have a soda or water with me."

"All right, fine," I laughed before walking away.

I finished my shift and joined the senator at a booth in the back of the bar. "I wanted to have a little more privacy. I hope you don't mind."

"No, not at all," I smiled, sitting down across from him.

"Do you like working here, Kendall?"

"Yes, I do. Everyone's nice enough and the tips are good. Do you like being a senator?"

"So you know who I am?" he asked, sounding genuinely surprised.

"Of course I do. I do have interests other than pouring and serving drinks," I replied, watching a sexy smile overtake his lips, reaching his pretty brown eyes.

"What are your plans for later on? After you've had enough of this job," he asked, sounding genuinely interested.

"I don't know," I replied honestly. I hadn't thought that far ahead. I was making good money, but there wasn't much left over at the end of the month. "Maybe post-secondary at some point. We'll see."

"There should be no 'maybes' when it comes to school. You're bright and will go far if you want to. Don't let hardship limit your potential," he said, his voice full of conviction. I couldn't shake the feeling that he had some experience with this, somehow.

"Easier said than done, sadly," I offered, taking a sip from my glass of water. "Don't think I didn't notice you didn't answer my question about your job. That was a good redirect."

"Redirect…" he repeated retrieving his buzzing cell phone off the table. "Good term." He sat silently looking at something on his phone. "I'm sorry," he offered, putting the device back down on the table. "These are times when I dislike my job."

"Why? What do you mean?"

"I've been in politics a long time and it's never really done. There isn't an off-switch. That makes it hard to focus on what I want to do. And right now, all I want to do is get to know the gorgeous woman before me. She deserves my undivided attention, and these are the moments when my job is frustrating. Otherwise, I love it."

My heart raced at his words, and I could feel the blush settling on my cheeks. I'd never had anyone talk to me like this before.

We spoke for hours. He was smart, kind and actually seemed interested in what I had to say. He was flirtatious, but not in an obvious way, and he somehow managed to make me feel special. I know that's odd, but it doesn't change the fact that it's true.

He told me had to go back to Washington D.C. for meetings and asked if I wanted to accompany him as his guest. At first I thought I'd misheard him; I mean, it isn't every day someone asks you to pretty much be a prostitute, but I hadn't misheard. That's exactly what he wanted. He was offering me a week long, all-expenses-covered invitation to join him. He said I could think of it as an all-inclusive vacation. At first, I couldn't help feeling deeply insulted and was all kinds of freaked out. I mean, you hear countless stories about women being charmed by beautiful men before they disappear never to be heard from again. I still can't explain it, but something about him made me say yes. In hindsight, it was a bold and reckless decision. It probably had something to do with my youth as well as some deeply-rooted daddy issues, but I didn't end up dead, and it turned out to be the decision of a lifetime.

For an entire week, I was whisked away to his house in Washington. While James worked attending committee and business meetings, I was living out my very own version of 'Pretty Woman' with money to shop all day and being escorted to fancy dinners in the evening. I kept holding my breath, waiting for the other shoe to drop because it was just too easy. Nothing this crazy could be this easy. I was convinced that there had to be something abnormal about this guy that I'd be subjected to – like maybe some crazy, weird fetish or some-thing. However, by day four, he still hadn't tried anything with me. No kissing, no touching, nothing. As messed up as it sounds, I had actually started to de-velop a complex because of the lack of action on his part. He was attractive and one of the nicest, most generous, most thoughtful people I'd ever met, and after four days I actually wanted him to try something on me. I mean, who asks a woman to accompany them for a week and then doesn't try anything? Like nothing, not one kiss or one arousing touch. Don't get me wrong, I can appreciate someone trying to be respectful, but this brought a whole new di-mension to the saying 'taking it slow'. Besides, I'd decided I wanted him, and if he wasn't going to make a move, then I was. To say I was mortified when he rejected me is somewhat of an understatement. I just couldn't understand why someone would bring me all the way to Washington, shower me in luxury and then turn me down for sex. I couldn't figure out if there was something wrong with him, or me.

James was suave and sophisticated, and had this uncanny ability to seduce a person without them even knowing he was doing it. I'd watched him do it for days, and it was a skill he had perfected. It didn't matter if the person was male, female, gay or straight, James could entice anyone into doing whatever he wanted. All he had to do was use that silky smooth voice of his and he could bend a person to his will, a skill I'm sure had a lot to do with his success.

The next morning, he surprised the hell out of me when he climbed into the shower with me. The things he made my body feel were unlike anything I'd ever experienced before. I remember afterwards feeling a little conflicted by what had just happened, given he'd turned me down the night before. After our first sexual encounter, I asked him why he'd said he wasn't interested in me, given the fact that he clearly was. I'll never forget his response. It taught me one of the most valuable lessons I've learned to date – 'Never let someone seduce you. You give up too much power that way. Always keep it on your terms. To seduce is an art form, and the truth is that seduction occurs on many levels whether it be physical, intellectual or emotional. Seduction is the enticement of behavior, and it's incredibly powerful.'

The next two days were filled with some of the most earth-shattering sex of my life. He taught me things that would make a porn star blush, and not because they were raunchy or kinky, but because of the way he did them. The way he looked at me made me feel like the sexiest person alive. The way he touched me made me feel like my skin was on fire, and the way he kissed me made my insides feel like they were exploding with pleasure. I wasn't a virgin when I met him, far from it, but the boys I'd allowed to touch me were just that – boys. James was a man.

On the final evening of that week he brought me to a private dinner party, with guests ranging from businessmen to politicians, no spouses allowed. There were, however, an abundance of attractive men as well as women much like my-self to keep guests entertained. James introduced me to a tall woman I guessed to be in her fifties. I remember thinking that she wasn't exactly beautiful, yet there was something about her that was completely captivating. Her whole de-meanor dripped elegance, and she moved with a distinct pose and purpose that could never be mimicked or taught. All eyes in the room followed her every stride, unable to look away.

"Kendall, this is Dominique Bourdeaux," James introduced, and I can still remember the nerves I felt when she spoke with her subtle French accent for the first time. No person had, or has ever since, intimidated me as much as she did.

"This must be the Kendall Daley I've heard so much about. Our James here thinks very highly of you, which is not something easily accomplished."

"It's nice to meet you," I managed to say, while shaking her slender hand.

"James was right about your beauty. So intense and unique," she said before turning her attention to him and running her well-manicured finger sensually along his jawline. "She really is darling, James."

"You know I would never waste your time, Dominique, mon amour," James replied, kissing her gently on the lips. The gesture was innocent but made me feel instantly awkward. They were clearly intimate with one another, and yet she obviously knew I was here with him, and that I had been intimate with him as well. It was incredibly bizarre. She focused her attention back on me and smiled, and I was in awe of how breathtaking it was. This woman was really something else.

"It was a pleasure to meet you, Kendall," she offered, gently kissing both my cheeks. "I very much hope to be seeing more of you." She leaned into James and whispered, "Let me know what happens. Au revoir."

I felt confused as I watched her long, raven curls bounce away from us. I couldn't understand why she would see me again, considering I was only going to be here for another day. It all became clear the next morning. That was the morning when James offered me a choice that changed my life.

I was in his bed, watching his naked body as he walked through the open doors of his closet. He crouched down and lifted what looked like a floorboard. Reaching underneath it, he pulled something out before replacing the floorboard, rendering the hiding spot invisible. He walked back over to me and handed me a large stack of cash, which I reluctantly placed in the palm of my hand. "Kendall, you have ten thousand dollars there. You can take this money, go back to Minneapolis and continue to live your life as you were. Or you can use it to make a fresh start here." I remember the intensity in his brown eyes as he handed me a piece of paper from the bedside table. The paper had Dominique's contact information scribbled on it. "Dominique's a good friend, and I owe her a lot. If you let her, she can help you make a fresh start."

"What are you talking about?" I asked, confused.

"Dominique runs a business here in D.C. that provides wealthy individuals with the company of interesting men and women."

"What is she, some kind of madam or something?" I asked, as my shocked eyes met his. I couldn't believe he was actually saying what I thought he was.

"Yes, that's exactly what she is," he answered matter-of-factly, as though it were no big deal.

"Let me get this straight; are you offering to pay me for the time I spent with you like I'm some kind of hooker? Or are you're asking me to agree to actually become a hooker for a living? If I wanted to sleep with people for money, I could have done that in Minnesota!" I exclaimed, hurt and angry that he thought so little of me. The irony of the situation wasn't lost on me. I had agreed to come here with him on a pampered 'vacation' for a week, so in a way you could look at that as being a kind of payment already, but still. For whatever reason, that large sum of cash was burning a hole in my hand, and made me feel cheap and dirty. I'd made it clear that this little getaway was a one-time thing and yet here he was asking me to pimp myself out on a permanent basis!

"Listen, Kendall, Dominique doesn't sell sex. She sells beauty, intelligence, personality and an escape from reality for those fortunate enough to pay for one. If you choose to sleep with a client that's your decision, but no one has the power to take away your freedom of choice."

"Well, isn't that just some modern fucking Geisha shit?" I stated, feeling totally baffled by the whole thing – it just didn't seem real.

"Kendall, you're so much better than the life you've been living. I knew it the moment I first saw you. This opportunity will allow you the chance to use your beauty and brains to make a lot of money, and if you're smart, you will be able to set yourself up for life. You can quit after a few years and start living the life you actually want, instead of the one you would be forced to live because of your circumstances. There aren't many other professions where you can make this much money in such a short time frame."

"Even if that's true, why would you do all this? Why would you offer me this great new life possibility? You're a senator, yet you moonlight as a madam's recruiter? It makes no sense. Are you in business with her?" I asked, wanting some answers. I'd been waiting for the other shoe to drop, and it was finally happening.

"No, I'm just a senator," he stated, pausing momentarily. "Truthfully, there was something about your eyes, those big, beautiful gray eyes that had me completely sucked in the moment you looked at me. That's an amazing skill to have, to be able to completely capture a person with one look. Beyond that, you're beautiful and charming, and carry yourself with an edge that somehow still manages to be effortlessly graceful without being vulnerable. You should own that and use it to your advantage. There aren't many opportunities for people like you and me — those born into a lesser life. We're more likely to repeat the negative cycles that we've lived than create positive ones. We have to take opportunities where we can, and Dominique can teach you skills that will serve you for a lifetime. It's not glamorous, I agree, but take it from someone who used to lead a double life as someone named Tyler and has experience working in that kind of profession that if you're smart, it can lead to better things. I'm not a recruiter, but I figured if you said yes, it would benefit Dominique and at the very least if you said no, you would still have given me permission to spend time with you, which was wonderful," he stated, gently running the back of his fingers along my cheek. "As you can imagine, not many people know about my past; I am entrusting that information to you. I want you to know that I'm not offering you cash to cheapen you, because I think you're an astonishing woman. I'd have been a fool not to want to spend time with you. I don't think you're the kind of woman who likes to take charity and the truth is, I like you. I care about what happens to you. Either way, I want to ensure you're taken care of."

Yes, that's how smooth James was. He could treat me like a hooker and make it sound all kinds of romantic. I still couldn't ignore that he'd done nothing up to that point that could be categorized as taking advantage of me. He hadn't talked down to me or treated me poorly, and had left every decision up to me. It was strange, but he'd been one of the most normal men I'd ever spent time with, and he'd provided me with one of the best weeks of my life. And even though I barely knew him, I had trusted him instantly. Potentially naïve on my part, considering getting people to trust him was a part of his job as a politician, but he didn't have to entrust me with a very personal detail of his past. Especially one that was this damaging to his reputation. Even though I felt conflicted, I couldn't help being tempted by the offer. If nothing else, he was living proof that with the right connections and enough money, a lot of things were possible, even reinventing yourself. I couldn't deny the appeal of that.

After calling Dominique that day, I've been living a double-life as an escort ever since. I'm Kendall Daley by day and Raina by night. I know a lot of people wouldn't approve of my current profession. I've battled with it myself from time to time. It's certainly not something I set as a life goal, but working for minimum wage and living paycheck to paycheck isn't something I'd dreamed about either. Alternatively, I probably could have found some rich boyfriend to take care of me, but that just doesn't sit well with me. Some people likely think that I've sold my soul, and maybe they're right, but it was my soul to sell. My life is still so much better than I thought it would be, which could arguably be viewed as a tragedy within itself, but it's the truth. Working for Dominique meant I only dealt with people who were vetted, tested and successful, such as lawyers, doctors, celebrities and politicians. I have the chance to travel the world and experience things most people will never try.

It wasn't always the easiest of transitions. I can't pretend that it hasn't caused me some inner turmoil – both on a moral and a personal level – but I have never been the type to dwell on things. I made the decision, and I've made the best of it. Still, the biggest question is whether people view me as a whore. Or better yet, whether I view myself as one. I'm not really sure how to answer that question. Beyond the legal aspects and definition of what I do, it really is a personal perspective. I wouldn't say I was or wasn't. I know it isn't really an answer, but I can't deny the fact that I've slept with some of my clients. It's not something I do all the time, but it does happen. Between school and working I don't have much time for an active social life, so when an attractive, well-dressed man comes around, I might let things go a little further. I don't like to sleep with married men, but it has happened, which isn't something I'm proud of. Most of the individuals, married or not, don't come to Dominique to hire people to sleep with. They're generally attractive individuals, or at the very least, incredibly rich and powerful ones who could have any number of willing participants sleep with them for free. They come to Dominique to hire someone who is attractive and personable, and who will listen and laugh at their jokes, but most of all, who will lavish the attention on them they want. I'm not paid to be a prostitute, I'm paid for my company, and my company includes a number of different things. I give clients what they need in that moment because that's what they're looking for, that and discretion of course.

I'm not sure if it's right or wrong, but life is full of good and bad decisions. Life is also incredibly hectic for all of us and especially for the clients I deal with, and sometimes they just need an escape. Is that wrong? Probably. Is it immoral? Yes. But the way I look at it, this is my job, and if one of my clients does something that he deems morally wrong, that's on him, not me. In my twenty-six years on this planet I've learned that life is messy and it isn't always perfect. But like James told me many years ago, sometimes you have to take opportunities when they are given to you. People can argue I could have been honorable and worked hard for minimum wage like so many others do, and they would be right. I can't argue with that, but I'd never have been able to go to university doing that. I would have stayed stuck in the unhappy life I was living and would have ended up God knows where. Dominique runs a clean operation, and I have always felt safe. How many others can say the same?

People can judge me, but until they've walked a mile in my shoes they will never understand me. I'm a survivor; I did what I had to do. Having said that,

I've been doing it a long time now and I'm ready to move on to the next chapter of my life. I put myself through university and completed my Master's degree in business. I'm in a stable enough financial position to start my own online clothing store and honestly, someday I'd like to meet Mr. Right and settle down. Who knows, maybe even have a family. But at the very least I want to finally live the life I've always dreamed of – the life I've been working for. I've already given my notice to Dominique and I have one last event to do before I'm officially out of the business. It's both exciting and terrifying, but this is what I've been working for since the day I started and it just feels like the right time. Life is about opportunities and doing things that scare you. The sky's the limit right now. Tomorrow will be my last evening as Raina, but for tonight, Kendall is going out for a much-needed night on the town.

Chapter 2

Kane

I've been sitting here, staring at the front of my brother's house for half an hour now and trying to make my way up to his door. I'm a U.S. Navy SEAL Senior Chief Petty Officer, who has been trained to withstand torture and kill a man in more ways than I can count. I've completed special operations missions in some of the most dangerous places in the world, and yet the thought of knocking on my own brother's door made me nauseatingly nervous. I don't get nervous easily, in fact, I was trained not to, and yet here I was, trying to process this very foreign emotion, which seemed impossible to master. I knew coming here was a mistake, but when he called and asked me to come see him while I was on leave, I couldn't say no. How do I move past this kind of nervousness? How can I process seeing a brother that I haven't seen in over sixteen years? A man that I hate for abandoning me to a foster home when I was seven, after we had already been abandoned by our parents? He was a man I hated for the life I discovered he lived, but most of all, he was a man I hated because I still loved him. It made no sense because I barely knew him, but logical or not, I felt like I needed him right now. My life was a mess at the moment and even though I was a grown thirty-five-year-old man who's been alone for a long time, I couldn't escape the fact that he was my family – my only family.

When he first started reaching out to me a few years ago, I wanted nothing to do with him. If nothing else, I admired his persistence. I don't know if it as a result of his years in politics, but when he wants something he can be quite stubborn to the point of exasperation, wearing me down slowly until I said yes. However, saying yes clearly didn't mean the battle was over because here I sat, unable to get out of my car. I noticed the front door open, and a man appeared in the doorway, watching me. Even though I hadn't seen him in many years, I knew it was him. We stared at each other for a long time before I finally gave up and turned the key in the ignition. My heart slammed against my chest with rage as I sped away from his house, as fast as I could. A part of me felt some sort of sick satisfaction for abandoning him for once, and another part was incredibly disappointed with my inability to face him. I found myself heading to a local pub to get a drink. I needed to feel numb right now because I hated feeling this way. Most days I hated feeling anything. Feelings go against all my training and everything I'm used to. Everything I'm comfortable with. I pulled up to a military pub; I needed the comfort of familiarity and my own kind right now.

"I entered the bar, "Beer?" the bartender asked as I sat down at the bar.

"Yeah. A shot of whiskey, too," I replied. I took a long draught of my beer and sighed audibly, as though it would somehow help release some of the anxiety I was feeling. I was starting to regret my leave of absence. I have no clue why I let my superiors convince me to take 'time off'. I worked a ton of missions, and I hadn't taken more than a day or two off in over five years. A part of me knew there would be no way I was going to be able to take six months off and remain sane, especially if I ever managed to see my brother.

Fuck my brother! If I could even call him that – somehow the word didn't seem to fit what he was. I ran my hands roughly through my hair before slamming down the shot. I needed to stop thinking about him.

"Rough day?" a soothing feminine voice asked. I looked up to find its owner, a woman with the most mesmerizing pair of gray eyes I'd ever seen. She sat down beside me with a sexy smile spread across her beautiful lips.

"You could say that," I replied, keeping my voice steady and taking another sip of my beer. The woman was stunning, but I wasn't quite sure I was in the mood for this right now.

"Can I buy you another beer?"

"I wouldn't waste your money on me. I'm not the best kind of company right now," I offered honestly, partially hoping that she would save herself from spending any more time with me. Nothing good would come of it.

"Correction, you weren't the best kind of company, but that was before you were spending time with me," she smiled, taking a sip of her own beer. "I'm Kendall, what's your name?" she asked while I stayed silent for a moment, contemplating if I wanted to engage any further. This seemed like my last chance to end this conversation before it started. My libido didn't seem to be taking this as an option. I was instantly mesmerized by how attractive she was; she barely had any makeup on and yet somehow managed to be one of the most striking women I'd ever seen. Even with her rather unconventional features; long dark cascading locks, straight nose, full cheeks and nice lips on what might be described as a somewhat oversized mouth. And of course, those eyes, the kind that would haunt your dreams. I'd be lying if I said there wasn't a string of dirty thoughts that crossed my mind after getting a good look at her outfit too; tight, dark wash jeans which showed off a great set of long legs, a slim waist and a snug off-the-shoulder gray sweater that showed off gorgeous breasts.

"Kane," I offered simply. "But don't say I didn't warn you about what shitty company I'll be."

"So serious," she teased with a pout that looked absolutely adorable. "I'm guessing by this seriousness that you're a military man."

"No offense, but considering we're in a military bar that's not exactly an earth-shattering guess."

"True, but that little twinkle in those otherwise very stern brown eyes tells me you're not the average kind of soldier," she said, causing my usually steady heart rate to pick up a little. I had a very high clearance and rarely talked about being a Navy SEAL, and that's the way I liked it. Talking about it only created more questions, so I preferred to leave the conversation off the table completely. Especially with a woman I barely knew, even if she was attractive.

"Did I hit a nerve?" she asked innocently, biting her bottom lip with a devilish gleam in her eyes. This woman was practically reading my mind.

"Well, you sure don't look like a soldier," I stated, trying to direct the topic away from me. I managed to sound uninterested, but it couldn't have been further from the truth, because at the moment this woman had my full attention.

"Probably because I'm definitely not military."

"What do you do then? You seem to like to read people as though you were one."

"Are you saying I'm right about you?" she asked, a grin tugging at her lips over the rim of her beer. She wasn't the only one with that skill – I knew how to read people too. In fact, I was trained to do it, and the fact that she could pick up on subtle cues so quickly told me she'd been trained, too. Maybe she was a shrink or law enforcement of some kind, although she could be in another field.

"So what is it that you do for a living? Sales?"

"Changing the subject again I see," she giggled playfully. "All right I'll bite. Yes… sales, that's somewhat accurate," she replied quickly, taking a sip of her beer. I could have been imagining it, but there was something off about the way she said the word 'sales' not to mention that she seemed uncomfortable.

"What's a girl like you doing in a bar like this then? I must admit, I would have pegged you as a wine drinker in a fancy place with some suits," I stated, finishing the last of my beer. I held up two fingers to the bartender who was looking my way for another order. It looked like I was staying put to chat with her. Hell, I was even ordering the next round. She was good.

"I do like wine, but I also like this place. My home is just around the corner, so it's convenient. Besides, I get my fill of suits in my line of work. Suits are highly overrated."

"I can't argue with you there," I laughed, feeling the same way. I wasn't the biggest fan of suits myself, considering they were usually the ones hiding behind a desk making decisions while I was the one with his ass on the line carrying them out. A certain family member of mine might also have a little something to do with my dislike for lying hand-shakers.

"Are you from around here?" she asked sweetly with a coy smile, batting her eyelashes at me. She was good at distracting, while asking personal questions that she knew I probably wouldn't want to answer.

"No, I'm here visiting someone, and once I deal with that I'll be leaving," I answered flatly, hoping she would catch on that I didn't want to talk about this subject.

"Must be a family member, or an ex-girlfriend gone bad," she offered simply, taking another sip of her drink. I didn't reply, mainly because I wasn't really sure how to — if I said yes, she would probably ask more questions, and if I said no, she would probably know I was lying. Silence was my best option at the moment because not even a pretty face like hers was going to get me to talk about my brother.

Silence ensued for a moment until she finally spoke again. "Please excuse me. I need to use the ladies' room," she said, and I watched her disappear through the restroom doors. I wasn't sure if she would come back, which was disappointing. I was angry with myself for not changing the topic or at least trying to make an effort. I'd managed to make things awkward when all she was doing was trying to be friendly.

The bartender walked over, leaning in to speak to me. "You're a lucky son of a bitch," he stated, confusing the hell out of me.

"Pardon?"

"You're a fucking lucky man! You're the first guy I've ever seen Kendall approach in here. It's usually the other way around, with very little interest on her end."

"What's her story, anyway?" I asked, more interested than I cared to admit.

"Besides the obvious that she's gorgeous, with a body that I would give pretty much anything to see more of," he offered, with pervy groan which annoyed the shit out of me, "I'm not really sure; she only comes in a couple of times a year. She's always sweet, and even though she usually has more than her fair share of male attention, I've never seen her go home with anyone. For a while,

I thought, or maybe I hoped, she might be a lesbian or maybe she was married. I guess not. One thing's for sure, she must like you."

"If that's true, I feel sorry for her," I said, unable to wipe the cocky smirk off my lips. I wasn't sure if it was the booze or just her, but as lame and immature as it was, my ego was currently heavily inflated at the thought of her wanting me. The bartender went back to the other end of the bar and a few minutes later, she sat back down beside me. Relief flowed through my veins, but I decided to play it cool and forced myself to wait a few seconds before I looked at her. I didn't want to seem too interested.

"Listen, Kane, I have an important question for you," she offered, drawing me into those intense eyes once again. "You're so tense and serious, and I'm not sure if..." she paused, taking a deep breath. She had obviously changed her mind about me. "I'm not sure if you'd be interested in shots."

"I'm sorry, what?" I asked, confused.

"Do you want to do shots?" she asked slowly, making sure to sound out every word.

"I'm confused," I offered honestly, unsure as to where the hell this was coming from.

"Well, confused is better than angry and moody," she teased. "I can work with confused."

I couldn't stop the audible laugh from escaping my chest. This girl was so random, but I was totally into it.

"So, Mr. Soldier Man," she said, leaning in so close that I could feel her warm breath on my face and smell the apple-pear scent of her shampoo, "yay or nay on the shots? But before you decide, you should know I'm no lightweight."

"Definitely, yay to it all." I smiled, wanting more than anything to spend as much time possible with this woman.

Chapter 3

Kendall

We drunkenly stumbled into my apartment, making out like two reckless teenagers. We'd clearly had one too many shots, but right now I couldn't care less. People might assume I'm slutty because of my job, but the truth was I rarely go home with guys. I especially didn't go home with ones that I barely knew, but there was just something about Kane I couldn't resist. I mean, aside from the fact that he was ridiculously sexy — there was a mystery and a vulnerability to him that had me totally bewitched. I found myself craving the closeness, desiring to know more about him. I sensed a little danger in him as well, which was apparent from those visible scars he wore on his skin like tattoos. Those brown eyes of his told me there were a lot of unseen scars below the surface, the kind of scars that a person only acquires after seeing and experiencing things most of us couldn't handle. I longed to find out more about that too. He was just so damned appealing.

My skin heated up against his hard body, which was pressed up against mine. I found my hands wanting to go everywhere at once and with each touch it was like a drug had taken over, and I'd lost control of the dosage. I couldn't believe this was happening. I never intended for the night to end up like this. I went out with friends to blow off some steam, but the moment I spotted him walking into the bar I couldn't take my eyes off him. The way he kept running his hands through his already untidy, dirty blond hair and how his dimples made his otherwise rugged features look younger somehow. And I'm not going to lie — his visibly hard body under his fitted sweater and jacket had done wonders to encourage my libido. So maybe I wasn't totally shocked we were in this situation. But the thing that had gotten me to approach him was his regal demeanor, which somehow screamed confidence and sadness at the same time. It was almost like he needed someone. Although it took a little bit for him to open up, there was an odd sense of familiarity about him that put me inexplicably at ease, like we were old friends or something.

I reached up his tall frame and wrapped my arms around his muscular neck as he deepened his kiss. I could taste the tequila on his breath as his tongue invaded my mouth. "Where's your room?" he asked breathlessly in between our flurried kisses.

"Down the hall to the right," I answered as he grabbed my hand and led me through the opened doors.

He stopped abruptly, staring down at me cupping my cheeks in his rough hands, "I didn't want to forget to tell you, you are so beautiful, Kendall."

My heart raced at his words, "You're not so bad yourself," I replied not letting him know how much his words were actually affecting me. They were simple ones in fact, and I'd heard them a hundred times over. And yet somehow the sincerity in his voice made them feel so raw, so real. I believed him and felt beautiful. Suddenly that's when James' haunting words sounded in my mind. Never let yourself be seduced. I was dangerously close to allowing him to do just that. I needed to keep my head on straight. I needed some distance from him to get myself in check before this went any further.

"Hold that thought, soldier. I'm going to go freshen up. Feel free to make yourself comfortable," I said, breaking our kiss and motioning to the bed. "I'll be right back."

I headed into my master bathroom and was a little surprised at the train wreck staring back at me in the mirror. To say I looked rough was a little bit of an understatement. I quickly washed my face and brushed my teeth before scooping up my breasts to perk them up a bit. Giving myself one last look, I headed back into the room. I stopped dead in my tracks, seeing a very scarred and bare-chested Kane passed out cold in my bed.

I couldn't decide if I wanted to sigh, laugh or melt at how adorable he looked. I quietly approached him, running my fingers down the lines of his face, admiring how peaceful he looked. I hadn't noticed how tired he was. As disappointing as it was, I decided to let him sleep. I removed his boots and covered him up with a blanket. I shut off the lights and crawled into bed beside him, enjoying the warmth of his body next to mine. It didn't take long for me to join him in sleep.

I woke up a few hours later to Kane's whimpering cries. I sat up quickly, wrapping my arms around him, "Shhh..." I said softly, gently running my fingers through his hair as he continued to cry in his sleep. My heart ached as he desperately wrapped his arms around my waist, holding me tight. I wasn't sure what the hell he was dreaming about, but whatever it was, it seemed to be causing him so much pain. It took about an hour, but he finally stopped crying and fell back into deep, peaceful sleep. I eventually drifted back into dreamless slumber as well.

✲

Kane

I tried to open my burning eyes, but my head was pounding so freaking bad that I couldn't. This had to be one of the worst hangovers I'd had in a long time, and that was saying something, considering I'd been consuming copious amounts of alcohol in the last couple of weeks. How long had I been sleeping? The last thing I remember was kissing Kendall and stumbling into her apartment like two sex-crazed lunatics. Kendall. My eyes shot open, and I found my arms clinging to Kendall's waist like a child. Had I actually slept like this? What the hell was wrong with me? How long had I been like this?

I glanced at the clock on her nightstand and saw it was almost 8:00 am, which surprised the hell out of me. I hadn't managed to sleep for more than four hours at a time for months now. According to the focused timeline I was currently replaying in my head from last night, it would appear as though I got close to a solid six hours. I couldn't remember if we'd had sex or not, but the fact that my pants were still on sort of answered that question. A mixture of annoyance and embarrassment shot through me; instead of coming here and having crazy sex with this incredibly sexy woman, I'd passed out and cuddled with her all night. To top it all off, the burning in my eyes had clearly been caused by tears. I fucking cried! Fuck!

I stared down at her sleeping figure. I could still smell her glorious apple shampoo under a heavy mask of alcohol. I'd been helplessly hypnotized by this woman all night, unable to look away. It was hard to put into words how beautiful, sexy and witty she was. Everything about her called out to me like a siren at sea, making me want to be near her. I've met women in countries all over the world and never has anyone affected me the way she did. It was that realization which caused an immense sadness to settle into my chest. I was a mess, and after everything that happened last night I couldn't imagine what she must think of me. She deserved better than what I was able to give her, and even though I knew in my heart that I'd never meet another woman like her again, I had to get out of here for both our sakes. I slowly removed my arms from her waist and shimmied my way up, quietly slipping off the bed without waking her.

She let out an adorable sigh before extending her arms out to find the blanket. I must have taken it off her accidently when I got up, so I carefully helped drape it over her, getting a good look at her killer curves. How could I have slept beside this woman all night and not had sex with her? I wanted to slap myself for being such a fucking idiot. Worst of all, I really liked her and wished that I could see her again. I wished things were different and that I wasn't so screwed up. I would have loved to get to know her better, but for now, getting as far away from her as possible was in her best interest.

I reached out, gently running my thumb across her beautiful pouty lips. She let out a dreamy sigh that made me rethink my whole plan. I wanted to change my mind and lie back down beside her, but I couldn't. I'd always be grateful for her company last night. I'd really needed someone, and I'd lucked out having a woman like her to spend it with. She'd been so amazing I had completely forgotten why I was in D.C in the first place, but I would have to deal with my asshole 'brother' at some point. The fact that I was abandoning her like a hypocrite killed me. I quickly threw my shirt and boots on, before grabbing my coat and rushing out of her apartment, feeling disgusted with myself. Fuck.

Kendall

My eyes fluttercd open, confused by the vacant space beside me in my bed. "Kane?" I called gently, reaching to the cold empty spot on the bed as though he'd suddenly appear. "Kane…" I called again, looking around the empty room and wondering where he was. I got up and checked the rooms in my apartment, but he was gone. I put some coffee on, thinking maybe he was doing that adorable thing some guys do in movies, where the girl thinks the handsome man left, but he actually just went out to get breakfast. Sadly, after thirty minutes it was painfully obvious he wasn't coming back. I couldn't believe he actually left! He didn't even bother to leave me a note or anything. What a douchebag! I wished so badly I'd gotten his number last night so I could call him to tell him off for being such an asshole.

I took a long, hot shower feeling unbelievably angry. I couldn't believe after everything that happened and everything he'd said last night, that he'd just left. I thought we had a connection, but I guess not. I was unbelievably thankful that we hadn't had sex. Worst of all, I'd believed him when he told me that he thought I was beautiful. I felt like such a fool. So many men have said sweet things to me over the years, but I never allowed myself to believe them. Say what you will about my business, but at least when a client whispers sweet nothings in my ear, I know it's business and not personal. Last night was totally personal for me, and for the first time in a long time I felt incredibly used and cheapened by someone I didn't even have sex with. This was absolute bullshit. Screw you, *Kane.*

Chapter 4

Kane

There I was sitting in front of his house again, not sure if I could actually get myself to walk up to the door this time. I'd thought about this moment for years now and yet I had no clue how to approach this. What would I say to him? A part of me wasn't sure whether I was going to punch him in the face. It was completely overwhelming. Fuck it! It's now or never. After a couple of deep breaths, I opened my vehicle door and exited, heading for his front door. Two men that I assumed were Capitol Police approached me. "Please stop, sir," one of them requested and I fought the urge to get into these guys faces. I'd finally gotten out of my car, and I wasn't in the mood for these guys stop me, or give me a hard time.

"I'm his brother," I offered bitterly, getting those words out for the first time in years. "He's expecting me." When they didn't protest any further, I bypassed them and continued towards the front door. My heart raced as I walked up the front steps, ringing the doorbell. The door opened moments later and a man I barely recognized answered it. "Kane? Is that you?" he asked, sounding stunned. For some reason I couldn't speak, so we just stood there staring at each other in silence. I thought for sure that I would be mad once I faced him, but honestly, all I felt was total and utter confusion. I couldn't move, and I couldn't think. This was really happening.

"Please come in," he offered after a few more moments of silence. I nodded, following him in without another word.

✹

Kendall

"Hello," I answered my work cell breathlessly.

"Raina darling, it's Dom. How are you? I've been trying to reach you since last night," she stated in her heavy French accent. From the day I'd accepted her job offer, she'd never used my real name.

"Yes, I'm fine. Sorry, I missed your calls. I was out, and I left my work cell at home," I replied. I never gave her more details than she needed to know. I didn't like for her to know too much about my personal life. I'd always worked hard to keep my professional and private spheres separate. I think that's the way she liked it, as well.

"All right, but are you sure you're okay? You don't sound like yourself," she pressed, sounding worried. Although I appreciated her concern, Dom was not my friend, she was my boss, and as long as I always showed up and did a good job, she has no business knowing anything.

"Perfectly fine, Dom. How can I help you?"

"Okay, d'accord, I'm just calling to confirm your attendance at the dinner this evening. James is expecting you," she stated, knowing full well I was still going. She knew this because she'd confirmed with me via text yesterday, so there was no need for this phone call. She obviously had other intentions, which I assumed would involve trying to guilt me into staying. She's been trying to talk me out of leaving the business from the moment I told her I was quitting.

"Of course I'll be there. I'd never let James down, you know that," I offered sweetly, not wanting to get into an argument with her. I cared for Dom, she'd taught me a lot and given me even more, but one thing I knew for certain was she liked getting her way, and unfortunately for her, so did I.

"Oui, of course, ma belle. I know," she offered, before pausing for a moment. "Listen, Raina, I wish you would reconsider. I think—"

"Dominique, listen, as I've already told you, I'm so grateful for all you've done. You've been so good to me, and I owe you so much, but I'm ready for a different life. I'm ready to move on before I'm no longer grateful but resentful. I'm sorry I'm disappointing you, but this feels like the right decision for me," I offered, trying to get her to understand that I couldn't let her wants dictate my decisions. This was my life.

"I know, my dear, I understand. I've often thought about what my life would be like if I had walked away years ago. At one point I thought about it, in fact in some ways, I still do," she offered, sounding sad.

"So what is this event again? What kind of lobbyist will I have the pleasure of entertaining this evening?" I asked, trying to change the topic. The last thing I wanted was for her to feel bad about her life on my account. If she was unhappy with her decisions, then she'd have to make the choice to change them.

"Well, officially it's Bring in the Light, to raise funds for mental health awareness and service expansion programs. Unofficially, it's a drug lobbyist, but you know I'm not into specifics. Ignorance is bliss."

"Ugh... that means lots of practicing lawyers," I groaned, annoyed. "I can't even pretend to be happy that this is my last event."

"Yes, I don't disagree, but many of them are tolerable. Besides, they are good business, and they adore you. It's also a good event for James' mental health platform," she answered in her typical diplomatic fashion. She always tried to keep a positive spin on everything. She always said it's the only way to get through life.

"Well, good business or good intention set aside, these events always bring out the worst in the shitty ones," I stated, then grinned, hearing her laugh on the other end of the phone. It suddenly dawned on me that this would likely be one of my last interactions with her. It was sort of bittersweet, but a little sweeter in my opinion.

"James has arranged for a town car to pick you up at nine at the standard location. He will meet you at the event."

That's odd, James usually always picked me up. "Oh... why the change from the usual?"

"James is bringing another guest tonight."

"You mean besides me?"

"Yes, besides you. This guest is special, a relative, so please bring your best tonight," she answered. I was beyond curious who this mystery guest was, but knew she wouldn't tell me even if I asked. Dominique wasn't one for gossip, especially if that gossip involved James. Her philosophy was if James wanted me to know he would tell me himself. They were loyal to each other almost to a fault. I often wondered why they weren't in a committed relationship, although I guess they sort of are. Sure they dated other people, but they remained the one constant in each other's lives.

"I always do. Tonight will be no different. I'll see you later, Dominique."

"Okay, but I won't be there until later. I'm getting too old to hang out at these parties all evening."

"Well, you and me both." I smiled, hearing a gentle snort on the other end.

"Au revoir, Raina," she said, sounding out my name. It was almost like she was truly saying goodbye to that person, and I guess in a way she was.

"Not quite goodbye yet, but very soon. See you later," I said, before hanging up the phone.

I walked over to my closet and picked out the very last outfit I would wear as an escort. I've been to a ton of parties for lawyers, so impressing them was easy; I knew what they liked. They like their women to be smart and witty, but not smarter than them. They liked women to be beautiful in a way that they could picture you attending court before screwing you. That meant tonight's outfit had to be an even mix of classy and sexy, with a healthy dose of ego-stroking. I scanned my outfits, pulling out a long-sleeved, low-back black fitted dress. With a half up-do and some black Mary-Jane pumps, this look should satisfy the masses.

"Well, this is it," I spoke aloud to myself and headed to my makeup table to get ready for what I imagined would be a long night.

Kendall

I exited the town car and stepped through the private country club doors. I handed my coat to an usher before walking into the Great Hall to find James among the hundreds of people walking around.

"Well, well, well, my dear Raina. I'm so happy to see you," Congressman Henry Kilman said, his bald head gleaming with sweat as he wore his signature creepy smile. "I was hoping you would finally agree to be my date this evening; however, I should have known you were already booked." Henry was the kind of guy who made me feel gross about my job. He'd requested my company a few times; however, something about him gave me the creeps. Because of that, sex was always off the table, which he was always dissatisfied with, so I never had to accompany him. "Let me guess who you're here with tonight… James?"

"Yes, that's correct. I'm here with James," I answered, glancing around trying to find a way out of this conversation as soon as possible.

"I figured," he sneered unhappily, his small, close-set eyes fixed on me. He and James were not friends in any sense of the word. "I hear you're leaving your line of work. I do wish we could have spent one night together," he stated, running his index finger along my shoulder in a circular motion.

"Sadly we could never agree on parameters, but yes, I'm leaving." I smiled, trying to take a step past him, but he shifted his body and blocked my path.

"Raina, my dear, I feel the need to tell you because I care for you. We find ourselves in troubling times. Your date – he's upset some people, and you should really be careful tonight," he warned cryptically. I had no clue what he was talking about, but I also had no intention of spending any more time with him to figure it out.

"Thank you for your concern, but James is a good man and has always been a gentleman with me."

"Well, let's just say he might be a good man, but good men still do stupid things that have serious consequences," he hissed, his face morphing into a rather menacing expression. I was irritated and getting incredibly uncomfortable.

"Yes, good men do stupid things, but I'm curious how you would know anything about it, given you aren't one of them," James stated from beside me. I
hadn't seen him approach, but I was grateful when he grabbed my hand and
guided me towards him in the opposite direction. "Now, please excuse us."

"Have a good night," I offered to Henry, hearing a string of insults directed
at us as we walked away, followed closely by one of James' staff members.

"Were you trapped long?" James asked, concern etched all over his face. "I'm
sorry, I didn't know you'd arrived. Otherwise, I would have met you at the door."

"No, not long, just a few minutes. He was warning me against the dangers of
being around you this evening. Apparently you're in trouble about something,"
I offered jokingly, but a part of me was a little concerned about the threat.
Something about it felt uncomfortably real.

"Yes, well, I'm always in trouble with men like him." James smiled, gently
kissing the back of my hand, looking unconcerned. "And before I forget, you
look absolutely stunning tonight."

I smiled at his compliment; even after all these years, James still managed to
make me blush. James and I had never been intimate again, and that served me
just fine, but we shared a strong bond. He was like family to me and probably
the one man I'd ever cared for. Well, that was before last night. I'd felt something
for Kane instantly, as odd as it sounds. Kane was obviously a serious error
of judgment on my part. "Thank you, Senator Clarke. You look quite dashing
yourself."

He smiled before turning to his staffer and saying something inaudible. I
glanced around the room, seeing a curious number of looks being directed at
us. Under normal circumstances, I wouldn't think much of it, but given Henry's
comments I found myself a little uncomfortable. "Raina," James offered, snapping me out of my daze, "I have someone special I want you to meet." He started
guiding me, his hand on the small of my back, towards the balcony.

"Yes. Dominique mentioned you brought someone, and I'm dying to know
who this mystery guest is," I offered, almost taken aback by how happy he
looked. I'd never seen him smile the way he was smiling now.

"My brother."

Did he just say brother? I was stunned into silence. I'd heard about a brother he took care of when he was younger, and who grew up in foster care, but I was under the impression that they were estranged. As we approached, there was something incredibly familiar about the tall, blond man who stood facing away from us. Oddly, the closer we got, the more nervous I felt because I knew this man somehow.

"Raina, my dear, I'd like to introduce you to my brother," James offered as the man turned to face me, "This is Kane."

I felt faint.

✺

Kane

I stared at Kendall, feeling incredibly confused. She wore way more makeup than last night and was dressed up, but I'd recognize those gray eyes and beautiful face anywhere. "Kendall?" I mumbled, bewildered as to why she was here and confused as to why James called her Raina.

"Do you know each other?" James asked, looking back and forth at us.

"We met last night at a bar and umm ..." I paused clearing my throat which had suddenly gotten very dry. "It doesn't matter..." I offered, hastily shaking my head before turning my attention back to Kendall, "What are you doing here?"

"I'm working," she whispered, looking incredibly pale, almost faint.

"What do you mean, you're working?" I asked, still not quite knowing what she was talking about. From what James told me this party was for politicians, lawyers, legal lobbyists. "You said you were in sales? Kendall, what's going on?"

She glanced around at us, clearly uncomfortable. "For the sake of this evening, please call her Raina," James requested, also looking around to ensure no one was listening.

"What do you mean, 'call her Raina'? What the hell is this? What's going on? How do you two know each other?" I demanded, feeling a spike in my temper. I was no longer stunned, but angry, and I didn't like feeling like I was missing something.

"First off, please lower your voice. Secondly, *Raina...*" he offered emphasizing the name, "Is my friend and companion for this evening. In order to protect her identity and safety we do not use her real name, okay?"

Okay? Was he kidding? No, this was not okay! I had no idea what was going on here! "If she's your date, why would she say she's working?"

"Because she is working," he replied awkwardly, offering her a small, encouraging smile. "She works as a companion for evenings such as this."

She works as a companion? He could dress it up all he wanted but that sounded an awful lot like a hooker to me. I was stunned into silence at the realization. Well, holy shit, she was a prostitute. "Are you telling me Kendall or fucking Raina – whatever the hell her name is – works as a prostitute and you've paid to screw her?" I asked, feeling both stunned and betrayed as I turned my focus back on to her. "How could you not tell me you're a whore?" I hissed at her angrily, watching her expression go from upset to insulted in two seconds flat.

I didn't care that I'd insulted her; this whole scene was too much! I'd felt like a jerk all day, worrying that I may have hurt her or that I'd let the girl of my dreams slip away, only to find out that she was a hooker and she was getting paid to sleep with my brother. What the hell?

Chapter 5

Kendall

I stared at him in disbelief, as his insult hit me like a slap across the face. How dare he act so high and mighty? He didn't know me, and he had no right to pass judgment on me. "First off, you can wipe that look of indignation off your fucking face. I don't make it a habit of telling every guy I meet about my business."

I took a deep breath, trying unsuccessfully to calm myself before beginning again. "James and I go way back, and he clearly stated he paid for my company. There was no mention of sex, you asshole. Not that it's your business, but I come to these parties and converse with people and help James. I never lied to you! I said I was starting a new profession, and I meant it."

"What do you want, a fucking prize or something?" he asked, sounding flabbergasted. "You lied to me! Had I known what and who you are, I would never have associated with you. And please, spare me the bullshit about not sleeping with clients. I'm not an idiot. I know what an escort is and what they do, Raina."

"Listen, I'm sorry if you're upset, but I didn't lie. We never even got around to last names last night! I didn't know you were James' brother!" I offered, a little ashamed that I'd spent the night sleeping beside this man, and I didn't even know his last name. "The fact is that I never lied to you. I told you as much as you needed to know, and besides, it's not as if you've been so forthcoming with your life story, so save the dramatic outrage. And not that I owe you an explanation, or that it's any of your business, but I don't make a habit of screwing all my clients. Or random guys I meet in a bar, for that matter. Now I'm sorry if you're angry or disgusted or whatever, but this is not the time or the place to have this discussion."

I could see James staring at us both, finally piecing together how we knew each other.

Kane shook his head furiously. "Well, hell, my bad – the next time I meet a woman in a bar I'll have us exchange our life stories, to make sure I'm not about to screw a prostitute. Then again, you did go home with me last night, so I should have known better."

"Oh really? That's how you're going to play it? I'm the slut for going home with *you*? You came home with *me*, remember? So save it, Kane! You're no better than me. And FYI, we never had sex, so you can go fuck yourself."

"That's the best thing I've heard so far. You know what, I shouldn't be surprised you know my brother so well, considering you're both whores," Kane spat, his nostrils flared with anger. I couldn't help noticing the hint of sadness in his eyes, though.

"That's enough, Kane. Do not call her that. You have no right to pass judgment on others, without knowing their stories or their struggles," James said, placing his scotch glass down on the railing before taking a protective step closer to me.

Kane's face quickly shifted to full-on rage. He looked as though he was ready to murder James, and I had a bad feeling about what was going to happen next. "You're going to defend her and talk to me about not passing judgment on others and their struggles? You don't even know me and my struggles, and I'm your brother!"

"I know that, Kane and I'm truly sorry. There are things that I'm not—"

Kane cut James off. "For years, I've dreamt up different scenarios about what you'd become and why you left me. I convinced myself that you were Superman. In my mind, it was the only explanation that made sense for why my only family would leave me! You can imagine my great disappointment when I finally found out at eighteen that you'd abandoned me to become a prostitute," Kane stated.

"That's not fair, Kane! I tried to take care of you after our parents left us, but I was young and barely out of high school, with no job experience and no money. For a year, I worked two minimum wage jobs. I was never home, and I could barely make enough money to pay the bills and put food on the table. Then one night, I delivered pizza to a beautiful French woman, and she changed everything for me. She gave me a job. Granted it wasn't a life I was necessarily proud of, but I was finally able support us, and I was even able to enroll in college. But between school and working, my days and nights were so hectic, and I was never home to take care of you. You deserved better than that. You deserved people who were there for you. You deserved a proper home. Having to give you to strangers to take care of you was the hardest thing I have ever done, but I promised myself I would work for a few years, finish school and come back for you. And I did that, I went back for you – but by then it was too late. You had a life beyond me, a good life, and I couldn't take that away from you."

"Leaving me with strangers does not mean you gave me a home! You had no right to make that decision for me! You were the only family I had, and you left me. Do you have any idea how hard that is for a kid?"

"Kane," James whispered, taking slow, shallow breaths, "I'm so sorry. Maybe it was the wrong decision, but back then I thought I was giving you the chance to grow up in a better place. I wanted to make something of myself, something you would be proud of. I contacted your foster home once a month to check on things and gave your foster parents money to help take care of you, but they weren't sure you could handle me being around too much. That day when you found me and asked me who Tyler was, I knew I failed you and I was ashamed of myself. I'm sorry Kane, but I can't go back. We can only move forward," James said, squeezing Kane's shoulder, trying to offer some kind of comfort to him. Kane stood motionless for a moment before walking away angrily, disappearing from the balcony inside the hall.

I'd never seen James look so depleted. "Are you all right?" I asked, putting my wine glass down on the terrace railing and approaching him. I placed his hands in mine, searching his brown eyes for a sign that he was okay.

"Yes, I'm all right. I wish things were different. I wish I had done things differently, but damn it, I can't change that now," he offered, taking his hands from mine and roughly rubbing his face in frustration.

"James, you did what you had to do. Right or wrong, you made the best decision at the time based on the information you had. Kane is a smart man, and although he might be an asshole, he will come around eventually. Right now his emotions are dictating his actions, which I imagine is challenging and somewhat foreign to him, given his line of work."

"His line of work?" James asked curiously. "What do you know about his line of work?"

"Not much, just that he's in the military. If I had to guess, though, I'd say SEALs, Special Ops," I offered confidently; I'd deduced his profession from the way he carried himself and the way he was so evasive about his work. Aside from that, his eyes seemed almost haunted — like when someone has seen things that are life changing in the worst kind of way.

"I know he doesn't talk about his work and from the little I know about him I'm guessing he isn't a 'pillow-talk' kind of guy, so why would you guess that?" he inquired curiously, which confirmed that I'd obviously guessed right.

"Oh, James, I'm hurt," I teased faking outrage to lighten the mood, and was relieved to see a smile tug at his lips, "For over seven years it's been my job to read people and uncover things about them that they might not want me to know. As you know, it's the best way to stay one step ahead them which better ensures you're giving them exactly what they really want and need. It's just good business sense for repeat customers. You're not the only one who's good at their job. Besides, I did learn from the best," I smirked, gently bumping my shoulder into his.

"You most certainly did," he chuckled. "I always knew there was something special about you." He frowned. "I'm really going to miss you."

"I'll be around from time to time; I just won't be getting paid, that's all," I laughed, picking up my wine glass and taking a big sip.

James and I glanced inside the ballroom at Kane, who was standing at the bar sipping his beer. His body was rigid with tension. "James, how did Kane find out about Tyler? You told me you covered your tracks after you left this profession."

"I did cover my tracks," he said with an audible sigh. "At least, I thought I did. I knew I wanted to be a politician before I quit being my escort alter-ego, Tyler, so I did things to protect my identity. I had some minor cosmetic surgery done to alter some of my features in hopes of minimizing people recognizing me. I graduated top of my class from law school, and I made the right friends. I thought I was safe. Kane tracked me down when he was eighteen. At the time, I was working for Senator Johnson. The senator happened to be very close friends with one of my former female clients, who'd put in a good word for me. My former client came by to meet with the senator about some charity event she was organizing at the same time as Kane came by. I innocently introduced them, and that's when it all fell apart. She made the mistake of saying something along the lines of 'I could have sworn he was Tyler, I mean you'. It was a stupid mistake, but it was damaging."

James picked up his glass of scotch and took a long sip before he continued. "It was true, too, at first glance, that Kane looked so much like my former self it had even taken me some time to get used to. No one but Kane and I heard her say it, I prayed he would just let it go as some innocent comment, but he kept asking about it throughout our lunch. When I tried to shrug it off, he knew I was lying and kept telling me that my face gave me away. After I returned to work he waited for my ex-client and asked her questions about Tyler. For whatever reason, she assumed he knew about my past profession. Kane confronted me that night. I can still remember the expression on his face and the disgust in his voice before he left. He joined the Navy a week later and for years we had no contact. I started reaching out to him just after meeting you, hoping we could try to mend our relationship. We exchanged the odd correspondence, but if tonight provides any indication, it's not looking promising that we can have an actual relationship."

"Well, this certainly turned out to be a much more awkward evening than we're used to," I joked before picking up my wine glass and draining it.

"You're telling me!" He snorted. "Bad enough to have a brother who hates me, but a brother who hates me and who knows your date personally is a new one, I must say."

"We didn't sleep together. Well, we did technically sleep beside each other, but we didn't do anything," I rambled, feeling all kinds of confused. I'd been so angry with Kanc this morning, but right now this morning was the least of our worries. To make matters worse, I clearly hadn't imagined the connection Kane and I had. He'd call me his dream girl. Kane had me totally enchanted last night, and yet here we were a day later, both livid and disgusted with each other. "I need another drink," I announced, after a few moments of silence. James nodded, and we quietly walked back into the ballroom.

"I should go talk to him," James suggested hesitantly as he watched his brother drinking at the bar. I couldn't decide if he was making a statement or asking a question.

"James!" A deep voice called from a few feet away. The voice belonged to Dylan Richton, chair and host of this fundraising event, who also happened to be a drug lobbyist. Sneaky how these events worked out; you can look like a saint while furthering your other interests. Dylan approached, and it looked as though he was in the mood to talk some business. That meant James would be trapped for a while.

"Dammit!" James groaned, looking incredibly torn. He was here to work and as much as I knew he wanted to run to Kane in hopes of fixing things, this really wasn't the time or place for them to try and mend their incredibly-strained relationship.

"Listen, you go deal with Richton. I'll check on Kane and once you're done, we can leave. You and Kane should talk. Sooner rather than later is probably for the best," I insisted, hating that I'd just offered myself up to go and talk to

Kane, who was currently the last person on earth that I wanted to converse with. Truthfully, the feeling was probably mutual.

James hesitated, looking over at Kane again. "Okay, fine. Thank you. I'll send my staff home, and I'll be done here in twenty minutes, tops. Just please, keep him here."

I sighed audibly as James walked away, and found myself wishing so badly that I could go with him. A wave of anger and anxiety flowed through me as I approached Kane.

Chapter 6

Kane

My body was still vibrating with anger; I ordered another drink before slamming the rest of the scotch in my glass. I had a feeling there wasn't enough alcohol in the world to make me forget the last thirty minutes. Not only had I finally confronted my brother about how I felt about him, but I'd also learned that Kendall – the cool, funny, smart, beautiful woman I'd spent the night with was, in fact, a hooker. And she may or may not be sleeping with my brother.

I let out an audible sigh as the bartender handed me a drink. I glanced over my shoulder, spotting James walking away from Kendall. I couldn't help staring at her. I didn't understand my luck; of all the girls in the world that I could have met and fallen for, why did it have to be this woman? Why did I have to fall for someone who worked as a hooker, and worse, someone who was involved with James? Fuck.

Kendall seemed to be heading in my direction, and I quickly spun back around, suffering an uncontrollable urge to get the hell out of there. Given the things I'd faced in my career, it was ridiculous that a woman could make me want to run and hide like a frightened child. My heart raced when she stopped a foot away from me and ordered a glass of wine. It was odd, somehow, despising this woman while all the while not being able to take my eyes off her. Even though my brain kept reminding me of what she was, that fact was slowly being overridden by the drinks I'd consumed. I found myself replaying last night's event in my mind. The way her lips had tasted and the way her breasts felt pressed up again me. Dammit.

I considered walking away from her until I heard a man's husky voice. "My dearest Raina, I'm so happy I found you."

I glanced over at the man, who had settled into the space between her and me. "Hello, Francis, how are you?" she asked. She wasn't doing a very good job of hiding the irritation in her voice.

"Better now that I've found you," he offered with an annoyingly flirtatious tone. "I called Dom to book you tonight, but sadly, you were already taken. Worst of all, I've been told after tonight you will no longer be available. I've wanted to take you out for years now, and it seems like such a waste for you to be here with James."

"A waste? How so?" she asked, taking a sip of her drink. It was apparent from her tone she was only humoring him.

"Everyone knows James' preference is to fuck the others and play wifey with you. So sentimental that he wanted to be your last date, although I could have shown you a better time for more money."

"James and I are friends. We have been for a long time, and he always shows me the wonderful time, with tonight being no exception," she offered. Her voice remained even, but I could tell he'd hit a nerve. Even though I was angry with Kendall for lying to me, I had to admit this guy was starting to get on my last nerves too. I didn't like the way he was talking to her and my patience was starting to wear thin.

"Listen, I won't beat around the bush. Although it's morally appalling, I would still like to get together with you. Even if it's off book, I'd be willing to pay you double," the guy propositioned, and I found myself gripping my drink glass tightly, fighting the urge to grab this guy's greasy black hair and slam my fist into his face.

"Thank you for that generous proposition, Francis. It is however, with great regret that I must remind you that I am, in fact, retired. No more bookings for me, but I'm sure Dom can offer you many other women who would gladly jump at such a fine opportunity," she responded, her voice sweet as honey while still peppered with sarcasm. I found myself doing an inner fist pump, because the thought of her sleeping with this creep – or really, any other guy –made me want to do bad, evil things.

"I'm not sure what the fucking problem is here, Raina," Francis stated, sounding irritated. "I'm disgusted by your profession, but I've heard you're the best and given that you're a whore, and I'm willing to pay you, I don't see the issue."

"Listen, Francis, you're drunk, so I'm going to let this little outburst slide. I suggest you step away now before you embarrass yourself in front of your colleagues," she requested sternly, and I found myself turning around to face them, waiting for the opportunity to take this guy out. I took a step towards him ready to grab him by the throat, but she waved her hand signaling for me to stop. I didn't understand this girl. This douchebag was disrespectful, and yet she wouldn't let me help her.

"I'm not going anywhere," he threatened taking a step towards her and grabbing her by the arm. She didn't flinch. She just stood a little taller, staring him in the eyes.

"Okay, let me get this straight, you are disgusted with me because of my profession and yet you insist this strongly on wanting to have sex with me?" She asked the question calmly and he nodded his head, a smug expression plastered on his face. "Ignoring the fact that this is completely and utterly contradictory, for the sake of discussion, let's discuss. What is it about my job that upsets you so much? Is it truly a moral outrage or a legal one?"

"The whole thing makes me sick. Anyone who has sex with someone who pays them is, at the very least, a disgusting human being. The fact that you've had sex with so many men is appalling."

"Just me? You're the one who wants to pay me for sex. Does that not make you equally disgusting?"

"No, because I'm doing the fucking – I'm not the one being fucked," he answered like a total idiot, who thought this was the most logical concept in the world. I'd like to say it was because he was clearly too drunk to make any sense, but I'm not so sure that was the case here. I think he was just a good, old-fashioned moron; one that I would like to punch.

"That's where I think you're wrong, because getting paid to do something is generally the better end of any agreement, is it not? Who knows though, Francis, maybe you're right. You're a handsome, rich and powerful man with a killer body, so I'm sure you've had your fair share of action with women. You'd know more about sexual intercourse than me," she complimented with a coy smile, running her index finger along his jaw. The action instantly released some of his tension.

"Yeah, you could say that. Ladies love me," he answered, peacocking like a fool over her compliment. He clearly didn't understand she was not only mocking him, but also manipulating the hell out of him. This woman was good, and this guy was a tool. I wasn't sure who in their right mind would hire him as a lawyer.

"I'm sort of ashamed to admit that I've been with upwards of twenty men, possible more, which I know is a lot more than the average woman, but I somehow doubt it's more than your number. I've seen the way women respond to you. You're incredibly appealing, and I bet even your clients hit on you and want to sleep with you, and rightfully so."

"You'd be right. I've had my fair share of them," Francis answered smugly, garnering the attention of a few men nearby.

"So by that logic, we've now established that were both arguably 'whores' by your previous definition. Now, if we look at the legal objection due to the exchanging of money—"

"We are nothing alike, you bitch," Francis sneered, cutting her off. He released his grip on Kendall, making her stumble.

"Oh, but I think we are. Tell me that you've never slept with any of your clients," she demanded, taking a defiant step towards him. When he didn't answer, she continued. "Judging by your silence I'm going to assume that you have had sex with someone, after they paid you for your services. So I ask you then, how am I the only whore involved in this conversation?"

"Go fuck yourself, Raina!" he snapped, his hands balling up into fists on hearing the nearby men snickering at their conversation.

"Oh, so sensitive, Francis!" she teased. "I suggest you run along now and have a good night. Also, maybe you should switch to coffee and water for a while, to avoid such scenes in the future." She spoke dismissively, grabbing her wine and walking past him to settle beside me at the bar.

"I have to admit, I'm impressed by how you handled that," I complimented her after we'd watched Francis storm away, his face ruddy with embarrassment. "But I still wish you would have just let me punch the guy. He was such a douchebag."

"Oh really?' she asked, one eyebrow arched in surprise. "He's a douchebag? Why?"

"Yeah, he is...' I offered awkwardly, not sure why I needed to explain myself. "I mean, he's an asshole for treating you like that. He called you a whore and yet insisted on propositioning you. It was ridiculous."

"Wow, suddenly you're such a noble and caring gentleman, and defending my honor? The truth is that you're not really in a position to judge him. In fact, he's a drunken asshole of a lawyer with an ego complex and probably a small dick; but at least he isn't trying to play it off like he isn't any of those things. You, on the other hand, should take a good look in the mirror before you start judging others, because not even an hour ago, you were quite content to call me a whore. The only difference is, Francis didn't spend the night with me, Kendall and didn't make me, Kendall believe that he liked me, before he made me feel cheap. So please, save your hypocritical outrage, because I have no use for it. James asked me to tell you he'll be ready to leave shortly."

I was stunned into silence as she walked away from me, disappearing onto the terrace. I stood there, trying to think of some sort of response, but I couldn't argue with her. She was right – I was a hypocritical jerk.

Chapter 7

Kendall

I inhaled the crisp air deeply into my lungs and exhaled it, willing the tension in my body to go along with it. As an escort, I've had to deal with many men and women treating me unkindly. The assumption that I was, first of all, cheap, and second of all, slutty, showed just how little those individuals knew about what my job really was. The people who judged me too freely were also the ones who would never know or understand. Having a work persona helped me maintain control over my work life, and I usually maintained a form of separation between my private and professional lives. James and Dominique had taught me a long time ago not to let anyone belittle me or devalue me. Truthfully, if I did my job properly, they would never have had the ability to take power away from me and cheapen me. I was always in control and believe it or not I did have power, but Kane was the first man I had ever let into my private life. He didn't know me as Raina, he knew me as Kendall, and this was totally uncharted territory for me. As Kendall, I hadn't had anyone make me feel as cheap as he'd made me feel in a long time, and I didn't like recalling how it felt.

The terrace being as quiet as it was, I could easily hear the footsteps approaching me from behind. Even with my back to the door I sensed that it was Kane. He stood silently for a minute, before he finally spoke. "Listen, Kendall… or I mean, Raina…" He sighed audibly. "Fuck, I don't even know what to call you. Fuck! I'm sorry I didn't mean that rudely. It's just... listen... I didn't mean to take my anger out on you, but I'm just—"

I turned around and silenced him with a wave of my hand. "Listen, Kane, it's fine. I understand you have a lot going on with your brother and probably others things in your life and..." I paused wondering if I should, in fact, let him finish. He would probably give me some form of an apology, perhaps even lie, explaining that he did care about me, but he couldn't get involved. Then in return, I would use the old cliché about being angrier with myself for letting him in. But overall, I just wasn't ready to hear the rejection he was about to subject me to, or to be honest with him about my own feelings. I didn't agree with him, but I couldn't be mad at him for whatever feelings or opinions he might have. Still, every time he opened his mouth he seemed to hurt me. I'd had enough hurt feelings today. "Let's just chalk up meeting each other as an experience we won't forget. Your brother must be done by now and will likely want to leave, so we should probably go back in."

I could tell he wanted to say something else but refrained; instead, he merely nodded and I walked past him, heading back through the doors with Kane in tow. I was ready to leave, and James' softening expression told me he somehow knew exactly what I was thinking.

"If you'll excuse me, gentlemen, I believe I will be calling it an evening. I have other plans to attend to," James stated, smugly gesturing over at me as I approached. I played my role well and sent him a coy smile, as I always did. We never actually had sex after these events, but I always made it seem as if we did. James often used this excuse to leave functions early. People were always so understanding of his desire to leave when they thought he was going to screw some young woman. That's exactly why I was his choice date for events; I played along with the life and that way, we both finished work early.

"James, you're leaving so soon?" Richton said, sounding almost panicked. It seemed like an odd reaction.

The expression on James' face confirmed he found Mr. Richton's reaction a little curious as well. "Yes, unfortunately I am. Let's do lunch next week, if you'd like. We can continue our chat then."

"No, you can't leave!" Richton blurted out. "I mean; I really must insist you stay a little longer." Richton persistence, after regaining his composure, raised further warning flags for me. Why was it so important for James to stay? Richton was an asshole, but not usually this pushy. He'd never had issues with us leaving early in the past. Kane took a step towards us, his eyes alert. Something about his stance seemed defensive, which had me think he was also getting a bad vibe. Kane barely knew this man, so the fact that he reacted this way had me all kinds of worried.

"No, not tonight, but thank you so much for your hospitality. This was a lovely evening. Raina, Kane, the car is waiting outside," James said, looking at us both and waving a hand towards the exit.

Once I'd grabbed my coat, and we were safely outside I glanced up at James, who appeared much more on edge than usual. This was odd, given his demeanor was normally so calm. "Was it just me, or was that a little weird?" I questioned, fighting the urge to look and make sure we weren't being followed.

The U.S Capitol Police, who served as James' security team, met us in the parking lot. I was incredibly happy that James was a senator, who often opted to have protection when he was in Washington. "Yes. To say he seemed fixated on me staying is an understatement. I'll feel better once we're away from here," James offered, glancing around nervously.

"James... what's going on?" I asked, concerned that we were in danger.

"I'm not sure. Now is not the time to discuss it, but we should call Dom once we're in the SUV to tell her we've left, and to warn her to stay clear of here," James answered. His cryptic response earned him a questioning glance from both Kane and me. He was being evasive, but whatever the problem was, it clearly involved Dom.

"Sir, O'Connor is headed this way with the vehicle. We should hurry," one of James' security men stated. I spotted the black SUV speeding through the parking lot and coming to a sharp halt in front of us. We had begun to hustle towards it when Kane barked out a single word. "Stop!"

"What is it?" James asked, confused.

"Someone's here," Kane warned, but before he could explain further, there was a flash of light followed by a groan and the sound of a car horn. Kane grabbed me by the forearm, and dragged me to hide behind a nearby vehicle.

"What happened? What was that?" I asked breathlessly, feeling panicked.

"A gunshot. Stay here! Don't move unless someone approaches you," Kane demanded, before he disappeared into the darkness. I adjusted my crouched position so I could more easily view my immediate vicinity. I could hear men fighting close by, but I couldn't see what was going on. I heard a second gunshot followed by a scream and a loud thump. My heartbeat pounded in my ears and I was so terrified, I barely registered what was happening. A strong pair of hands grabbed me from behind and dragged me from my hiding spot. I screamed as loudly as I could, but the man slapped me hard across the face, sending me stumbling backwards into a vehicle.

"Get her out of here! Don't trust anyone!" James shouted from inside the vehicle. I suspected that he thought Kane was nearby, and his words were directed towards him. One of the men in the vehicle reached over and smacked him hard across the face with the handle of his gun. James let out a muffled moan, before blacking out, his head slumping forward in the seat. "Where's the man you were with? Did that coward leave you all alone?" The man questioned, an evil smile spreading across his lips. I had no clue where Kane was, and even if I did, I wouldn't have told this asshole. I knew one thing for sure: Kane wouldn't leave me here alone, he must be nearby.

"Russ! We got the senator, and all the security detail is dead. We have to bring the girl, too! We have to move!" A nearby man shouted at my attacker as he wrapped his arm around my waist and dragged me towards a blue GMC SUV with blacked-out license plates.

"Let me go!" I shouted, trying to free myself. I dug my heels into the asphalt, in an attempt to gain what little traction I could. I looked around frantically as we inched closer to their SUV. I knew if they got me in there, I'd be doomed. I heard a loud gasp followed by what sounded like a loud twig breaking and suddenly, my assailant released me. I looked up to find Kane standing over my attacker's dead body. I could tell by the distorted way the guy's neck looked, it had been broken.

Sirens rang out from nearby and Kane grabbed my hand, dragging me over to a nearby bush, and we settled into a crouched position. "Shouldn't we be running towards the sirens or something?" I whispered=. Why were we just sitting here?

"No, not yet" he answered, watching intently as the blue SUV stayed in the same position, even with the police cruiser approaching.

"Why aren't they leaving?"

"That's a good question. Let's wait and see," Kane offered, pulling me a little closer to him as we watched the scene unfold. A squad car pulled up next to the blue SUV. The police officer on the driver's side of the vehicle got out and walked over to the passenger side of the blue SUV.

"Where's the woman?" the cop asked, which I gathered meant me.

"She got away, but she wasn't alone, there was some other guy with her."

"Fuck, Marty! This was supposed to be clean and discreet!" the officer said, running his hands through his hair angrily.

Have you found out where that bitch lives yet, at least?" Marty asked angrily, lighting a cigarette. The one named Marty asked, lighting a cigarette.

"No, and no luck on the lists yet, either."

"Dammit!" he hissed roughly, "Well, we'll see what Mr. Senator here is willing to share. Hopefully, it's more than that French bitch. Clean up this mess. We'll talk soon." And without another word, the SUV sped off.

"So the cops are involved in all this?" I asked in disbelief. What the hell was happening here?

"Looks like it. Which means we won't be able to rely on them for any help. What the hell has James gotten himself into?" Kane asked. "We should get out of here." He grabbed my hand, and we took off running through a wooded area, getting as far away from the parking lot as possible.

After we ran for what seemed like forever, we reached a bar parking lot. Kane stopped abruptly. "Stay here. I'll be right back," I wanted to protest, but I was too tired and out of breath to get the words out. Within moments, Kane pulled up beside me in a green Toyota Camry. "Get in, Kendall."

I stared at him in dismay. "Did you steal that?"

"Seriously? After everything that's gone on tonight, getting into a stolen vehicle is where you draw the line? We don't have time for this! Get in," Kane spat, sounding exasperated. I reluctantly got into the car and he sped off.

"They took James…" I whispered after a few minutes.

"Yeah, it appears as though they came for him and you, too," Kane answered, never taking his eyes off the road. "Any ideas why?"

"No clue at all," I answered. I was bewildered by the events of the last half hour, but I noticed Kane's eyes glance my way, as though he wasn't sure I was telling the truth, "Honestly, I have no clue. I'd tell you if I did!"

He nodded, seeming satisfied.

"I wonder who called the cops?" I questioned.

"I did, using one of James' security personnel's cell phones. That's why it took me a couple of seconds to get back to you when that scumbag took you. Calling the police was originally intended to get help, but once I heard Kane's warning, I was hoping it would at least buy us some time to escape from whoever the hell those guys are. Although I wasn't expecting what appears to be dirty cops, my guess is that they were close by on standby, waiting for this to occur and responded to the call before anyone else could, which is why they showed up so quickly and without backup. I know professionals when I see them, and these men were professionals. They seem to have the added bonus of having cops on their side, which means whoever orchestrated this must have deep pockets and a lot of power. They came for James and you, and until we figure out what the hell is going on and why, we need to be careful and smart."

I was trying process everything that was going on. This whole thing was completely insane. How had I gotten in the middle of it? What did they want with me? One name came to mind, Dominique. "We have to get to Dominique," I stated frantically. Kane glanced across at me, looking confused.

"Why?"

"When things started getting weird, and I asked James about it, he said he needed to contact Dom and warn her to stay clear. Then that man back there mentioned a 'French Bitch'. It can't be a coincidence. Dominique must know something about what's happening. I know where she lives."

Kane was quiet a moment, thinking, "Fine, I don't like this idea but we don't have much else to go on. We'll ditch the car a few blocks from her place."

Kane and I hiked my dress up and climbed over the fence leading to Dominique's backward. Kane insisted on staying hidden, so we wouldn't draw any attention to ourselves. The lights were on inside the house, but there didn't appear to be much movement. The back door was ajar.

"Wait here, I'm just going to check the house quickly."

"No! I'm not staying out here by myself. I'd rather be in there with you. I'll stay back. I won't get in the way. Please," I pleaded. He let out a deep sigh before nodding his agreement.

"Be careful and quiet and don't touch anything. We don't want anyone to know we were here," Kane insisted as we made our way through the back door. The house had been ransacked. Whoever had been here, had obviously been searching for something. I walked down a hallway which led to a series of rooms, including what must be Dominique's office. As I slowly crept through the doorway I was taken aback by all the misplaced and broken furniture. There were papers everywhere and there appeared to be bloody handprints on the wall. My pulse quickened in terror at what I might find on the other side of Dominique's desk.

"Oh my God! Dom!" I cried, running towards her motionless, blood-covered body. I wanted to help her, but there was so much blood I didn't know where to start or what to do.

"Don't touch her! Don't touch anything!" Kane insisted, as I shot him a pleading look.

"I can't just leave her like that!" I said. Kane leaned in close to Dominique, avoiding the pool of blood that surrounded her. He crouched down and reached forward, gently checking her neck for a pulse.

"I'm sorry, Kendall, she's gone," he offered, wiping the spot he'd touched with his sleeve. My vision suddenly blurred. I felt as if I wanted to sob but for some reason I couldn't; in fact, I could barely think straight. Kane straightened up. "Are you okay?"

"Honestly, no," I answered, having a hard time catching my breath. I stared at Dominique's body. I'd only spoken to her this morning, and now she was gone. Everything had changed.

He nodded in understanding. "Kendall, we need to get out of here. We should leave the same way we came in, before anyone realizes we're here. My guess is someone might be coming by here at some point – cops or otherwise – and we don't want to be here when they get here. Once we get downtown, we'll take a cab to your place for now."

I nodded, willing to follow his lead for now. Truth was, I had no idea what to do at this point. I'd almost been kidnapped, Dominique was dead, James was who knows where, having who knows what done to him and for all I knew there were trained killers after me. I needed help — I needed Kane. He carefully led me out of the house, helping me to walk. I felt so unbelievably lost. Before long we were over the fence once more, and we disappeared into the night.

Chapter 8

Kane

We reached Kendall's apartment, and I immediately started checking for any signs of tampering. I sure wished I hadn't left my gun locked-up back at the shitty apartment I was renting a couple of hours away from here. For some reason, I hadn't thought I would need it. How silly of me, right? Besides, the idea of having it in my possession while dealing with my estranged brother had seemed like a bad idea. In hindsight, I'll never leave it at home again. Regardless, I would have to make do. I took out my RF pen and began scanning the area for any bugging devices as Kendall sat motionless on the couch, still wearing the dirty and blood-trickled clothing. I knew very well how badly her mind and body would be battling through the stages of grief and shock. She'd been attacked, witnessed horrible violence, almost been kidnapped which would have resulted in God knows what, and discovered one of her friends had been murdered. Tonight was probably one of the worst nights of her life, and it would likely haunt her for the rest of her days. It was a horrible thing to have to live through, but I was almost certain this wouldn't be the last bad night she had to deal with in the near future. These men had been hired by someone, to find and kill my brother, Dominique and Kendall. They'd ransacked Dominique's place, but based on what that dirty cop had said, hadn't found what they were looking for. I wasn't sure if Kendall was collateral damage, or if she knew more than what she was saying. Regardless, whoever was behind this thought she did know something, and they wouldn't stop until the job was done.

I had to figure out what our next move should be, because odds were that they had already ransacked, or were in the process of ransacking James' house. I wasn't sure how long we had until they had Kendall's address. I didn't know how close she and my brother were, and that information would affect how quickly these killers might discover our location. I needed that information to try and figure out what to do next.

I walked over to Kendall and crouched in front of her, trying to make myself as small as possible, so as not to intimidate her further. "Kendall..." I said softly, trying to get her to focus, "Kendall, can you look at me, please?"

Her sad eyes met mine and for a second, I was overcome with compassion. I wanted so badly to bundle her into my arms and hug her for as long as she needed me to, but my training quickly pushed all those emotions out of the way. I needed to focus. "Kendall, is this apartment in your name?"

"Yes," she answered in a small voice.

"Does Dominique have anything in her records, with your name and address on it?"

"No, she always referred to me as Raina for business purposes. She never kept a file, or records of addresses or anything, because she didn't need to. I was always picked up in front of a hotel a few blocks away, and we never spoke outside of work. Everything was done over the phone. Even my payments came by electronic transfer."

"What phone did you use?"

"My work phone, Dominique..." she paused a moment at the mention of her late employer's name, "she gave us all new burner phones on a bi-monthly basis," she stated, grabbing her purse and pulling out a black cell phone.

"Give it to me, please." She handed it to me and I dropped it onto the floor, stomping on it to smash it. She watched intently as I strode into the kitchen and placed the remains of the phone in the sink, running water over them. I wasn't sure if they'd thought to track it, but I was hoping they hadn't gotten that far yet. I walked back in the living room. "So, you never use your personal cell phone for work? Did James ever call you on it?"

She shook her head. "No, never."

"What about staying here? Did James ever stay here? Would anyone have any way of tracing him back to this location?" My chest tightened uncomfortably, as if someone had kicked me. Even after everything that had happened tonight, the thought of them together left me both hurt and angry.

"No. It's not that kind of relationship," she snapped, her eyes practically scorching me with unconcealed irritation.

I nodded, not really certain what she meant, but the last thing I wanted to do was get into the specifics of their relationship, "Okay then, we're going to go with the assumption that they don't know where you live yet. It's late, and I think we've both dealt with enough tonight. We should be safe here for now, and we can leave first thing tomorrow morning." She nodded her agreement. "For now, I'm going to suggest you go take a shower."

Noticing the blush which settled on her cheeks, I figured I should clarify. "To get the blood and dirt off of you. You'll feel a little better once you're clean. Then you should pack a bag and try to get some rest."

"Yeah, okay," she said, glancing down at her dirt-covered legs and hands. "What happens after that? Where will we go tomorrow?"

"The first thing is to try and figure out what they're looking for and get it before they do. Then we try to arrange a trade, or go to the authorities if needed. But we obviously have to be very careful about who we deal with in the local police force. We'll need to find someone we can trust. I have a few friends here in Washington I'm going to reach out to and see what they might know." I was pretty sure Jeremy still worked as a Naval Intelligence Advisor at one of the bases in Washington. He would be a good place to start. I watched Kendall thinking everything over. "Is there anything you can think of that might be linked to this situation? Anyone you know who would want to hurt James and Dominique, or you, for that matter?"

"No, I've been trying to think, but nobody comes to mind. I wasn't exactly in the inner circle with James and Dominique. James is a senator and a good one at that, he's very cunning and influential, so I'm sure there's a list of people who might not like him for one reason or another. My guess is James confided something in Dom, or she was involved in whatever was going on. As for me, I'm at a total loss as to how I got roped into all this," she stated.

I trusted her. Although I didn't know her well, Kendall didn't strike me as someone who would be stupid enough to withhold important information given this situation. I believed if she'd known anything; she would have shared it.

"Okay, let me know if anything jumps out at you. I need some time to think. Tomorrow we'll figure out our next move. In the meantime, I'll reach out to some of my contacts."

She got up and headed toward the bathroom. Stopping in the doorway, she slowly turned back to face me. "I wanted to say thank you, for saving me tonight. I appreciate all your help but... if you want to leave, you can. I won't blame you. I can go on the run for a while and try to figure things out. You don't need to be involved in all this... this... madness. I know you and James weren't close, and it's not too late for you to walk away. You didn't ask for this," she said earnestly, sounding both incredibly brave and vulnerable at the same time. She was right, I had no real relationship with my brother, or with her. I could leave and never look back, but it wasn't in my nature. I couldn't leave her exposed and vulnerable like this. And even if he was a shitty brother, I couldn't leave James to rot and die somewhere.

"You didn't ask for this either. Besides, they saw my face, so whether I like it or not, I'm involved now." I answered honestly, unsure whether they would come after me. Of course, I'd been trained to protect myself and as long as I was working in the SEALs, I was better protected from being identified by any system. Especially not without alerting my superiors at the very least. Given my rank and my skill-set I was very important to them, which warranted additional protection at times. Sometimes it was useful knowing how to be a ghost.

"Well then, thank you again, but this time for staying. I'm grateful," Kendall said as she walked through the doorway, closing the door behind her.

I found myself smiling, an unusual reaction given the circumstances, but I couldn't help it. It was odd to actually be thanked for doing what comes naturally to me — being a fixer, an investigator, a protector, and a soldier. What I was doing right now. Everything about this was like the job I did every day, and honestly, as sick and difficult as my job can be at times, I'm good at it. At least, I was, before the incident happened – but then something changed in me. In fact, everything changed for me. I wasn't sure what was driving me right now. Was it the subconscious desire to find and save a brother I hated? Or was it protecting Kendall? I wasn't certain, but for the first time in a long time, even among all this chaos, I felt like myself again. Protecting the innocent was an important job, one which I took very seriously. I would do anything needed to see this through. I just hoped whatever happened in the immediate future wouldn't leave me even more broken than I already was.

Kendall

I did feel a little better after a long shower. I hadn't even realized how dirty I was, until Kane pointed it out. I dressed in a pair of jeans and a t-shirt while Kane jumped in the shower. It felt amazing to be clean after the horrible events of the past few hours.

In my bedroom, I did as Kane had requested; packing a bag of necessary items to bring with me. I went back to the living room and found a bowl of spaghetti waiting for me, which was nice of him. I hadn't been hungry, but now that the food was in front of me, I ate everything and fought back the urge to lick the bowl clean. I settled back on the couch, which Kane had backed up against a curtained window and now faced the front door. I turned on the television at a low volume, trying to distract myself from an ever-increasing sense of fatigue and the fact that there were men out there trying to kill me. Not exactly the easiest thing to 'forget'. Kane walked out of the bathroom wearing his suit pants and a tight white undershirt, leaving very little to the imagination. It did a far better job of distracting me than the television had. He glanced over, catching me openly admiring him, and I swiftly diverted my gaze, staring at the television with all my might. I noticed a smirk tugging at his lips when he sat down beside me, with my laptop in hand.

"Is it okay if I use this?"

"Yup, yup... yup. It's fine," I muttered, thinking that I sounded like a complete idiot. I tried to ignore the fact that he was sitting beside me, but memories flashed of us kissing last night. My breath hitched and then sped up as the thoughts ran on repeat in my mind. It was absurd how confusing the human mind was. How could you go from thinking about potentially being assassinated and seeing people die, to suddenly thinking about sex? If someone had told me they were thinking of sex when they were in my position, I would probably have pegged them as insane. It was completely morbid and yet here I was, unable to control it. There must be something seriously wrong with me.

"I hope you don't mind me sitting here," he said, not taking his eyes off the laptop screen. "It's just easier to react quickly if we need to make a run for it. Plus, this window gives me a good view of the front of the building."

"Oh umm... nope, that's totally fine," I muttered again, suddenly incredibly aware of the heat of his body next to mine.

He furrowed his brow. "Are you okay, Kendall?

"Yes, I'm fine. So what are you doing on there, anyway?" I asked, feeling my cheeks getting hot as I tried to change the topic. He cast me an odd look, and it suddenly dawned on me that he probably didn't want to tell me. "I'm sorry. I was just curious, and I don't know... Sorry," I said, embarrassed. Grabbing a couch cushion, I placed it down on the couch's armrest. I laid my head on it, wishing I could suffocate myself. It wasn't as if we were friends or anything. Even though we'd gone through a lot together tonight, and we'd almost done the horizontal mambo the previous night, we weren't friends. We were definitely not close enough for me to be so nosey. I focused my attention on the television screen again; not really watching it, but it provided a nice distraction. The mental and physical exhaustion from the night was hitting me full force.

It didn't take long for my eyelids to start feeling heavy, and I knew it was only a matter of time before I fell asleep.

"I'm looking online to see if there are any issues or names that stand out in James' inner circle. I'm trying to find out if anyone seems like they might target my brother," Kane offered, a minute or two later.

It was nice of him to be so open, but I was exhausted and no longer seemed to have the energy to care. "Oh, that's a good idea," I said sleepily. "Let me know what you find."

I heard a sigh escape his lips. "You're tired. ? You should go to bed."

"No, please," I pleaded opening my heavy eyes from sheer panic. "If it's all the same to you, I'd rather stay here. I don't want to be alone right now." He hesitated a moment, but nodded. Relief washed over me as he focused his attention back on the laptop screen. I closed my eyes and listened to the clicking of the keys from the keyboard for a few minutes, before I was pulled into a torrid, nightmare-filled sleep.

☼

Kane

My eyes snapped open in a panic as I looked around Kendall's empty living room. I quickly jumped to my feet, rushing from room to room, calling her name. How long had I been asleep and where in the hell was she? Had they taken her? Why hadn't I heard anything? Surely I would have heard someone come in. I walked over to the front door and found the deadbolt still latched. There appeared to be no forced entry. How could I have been so irresponsible and fallen asleep? I'd barely slept for weeks with no ill effects, and yet two nights with this woman and I not only passed out before having sex, but now, when I was supposed to be protecting her, I'd passed out again. I inspected the apartment, noting that her purse and cell phone were gone. If someone had gotten in here and abducted her, they wouldn't have grabbed her belongings. She must have left on her own. Had she run away?

I walked over to my cell phone and noticed a handwritten note tucked beneath it.

I'll be back soon. – Kendall.

I'll be back soon? What the hell was wrong with her? We had hired killers after us, and she goes off gallivanting somewhere and leaves this ridiculously vague note! What if they've figured out where she lives, and they were outside waiting for her? Maybe they've taken her already! Fuck!

I suddenly felt completely helpless. I had no idea where to start looking for her. Should I go out there and start searching? What if she came back and they come for her when I'm not here? *Dammit*! I glanced at the clock; it was nine in the morning. If she wasn't back by ten, I'd go out there to search for her. I went into the bathroom and splashed some water on my face, taking a few deep, calming breaths. The woman was driving me crazy! I was a trained soldier who could remain calm in almost every single situation imaginable, yet somehow, Kendall managed to get under my skin like no one else could.

I heard the door creak open, so I quietly positioned myself in the doorway of the bathroom. I would be able to get a clean jump on whoever was here; I just had to wait until they were close enough for me to overpower them. One, two, three... I leapt out from the doorway and tackled the trespasser to the floor.

"Ow!" I recognized the voice. It was a female, and she sounded like Kendall, even though she didn't look like her. "Get off of me!" she demanded, struggling beneath my weight.

"Who the hell are you and who sent you?" I demanded, easing up a bit to allow her to talk.

"It's Kendall, you moron! Get off me!" she shrieked, wriggling frantically. I quickly moved off her and a second later, had her stormy gray eyes glaring at me. "What the hell is wrong with you? You could have killed me!"

"Oh, please, calm down. If I'd wanted you dead you would be; besides, where in the hell have you been? You just left without saying a word!" I retorted, trying not to notice how amazing her freshly-cut hair looked. She'd had it shortened to chin length, and dyed blonde.

"Obviously, I went to get my hair done," she fumed, pointing at her head. She rolled her eyes, as if I was a total idiot. "Besides, I left you a note!"

"Oh, you mean the one that said 'I'll be back soon'? Oh, my bad, that was really fucking helpful," I growled, trying to keep my temper at bay. "What's the point of all this anyway?" I asked waving my hand at her hair.

"Well… you were sleeping when I woke up. I couldn't go back to sleep, so I started thinking, and I got the idea. I figured they were looking for me as a long-haired brunette, so it might be helpful to change my appearance. You know like a disguise…" she offered, her cheeks turning a deep shade of pink.

"Oh, that's just great! You go wandering around to find some random hairdresser to do your hair, when you have people trying to kill you! That's a brilliant plan, Kendall!"

"First off, my friend cut my hair. She's a hairdresser and lives a block from here. Secondly, I thought it might help. You know, to stay under the radar or something… They do this sort of stuff in the movies all the time!"

I threw my hands up in the air. "Oh my God! Are you fucking serious? You're seriously going to kill me here, with the fact that you're taking advice from movies now," I stated, completely outraged. But the truth was, a part of me knew it was actually a good idea. Her new look paired with her ripped jeans, converse sneakers and a baggy sweater did in fact, look very different from her usual brunette goddess self. This makeover might actually help us, but I was on a roll, and I couldn't let her know that. Plus, it didn't excuse the fact that she didn't seem to understand how serious this situation was. If she did, she wouldn't have left. I couldn't keep her alive if she kept making reckless decisions. This was not how things were going to work; I couldn't operate this way. "From now on, you tell me everything, okay? You tell me who you're talking to, who you're with and where you're going. Got it?" I demanded, practically snarling. "Grab your shit. It's time to go," I ordered angrily, stalking over to the coffee table to grab her laptop. She didn't argue, but the slump in her shoulders told me she was feeling a little depleted. I felt like an asshole for treating her like that, but we didn't have time to deal with it right now. We really did have to get out of there.

Chapter 9

Kendall

As I followed Kane down the street, I realized my makeover was an epic fail. I don't know what I expected, but him being such a dick about it certainly wasn't the reaction I thought I would get. I ran my fingers through my hair, surprised at how light it felt. He was mad I hadn't told him where I'd gone, and I guess I understood his annoyance, but at the same time, I'm not a total idiot and I wouldn't put myself at risk. Not on purpose, anyway. Regardless, I still thought it was a brilliant plan on my part. Then again, having psychopathic assassins trying to capture and kill me has never been a worry of mine, so what did I know? Even if Kane was right, I wouldn't give him the satisfaction of knowing it, especially because he was such a smug jerk about everything. His phone rang, distracting me, "Yeah it's me…" he said, answering the call. "Yes, the sooner, the better… no, public. Sorry, but it has to be public. All right, nineteen hundred hours at L. Memorial."

He disconnected the call and placed his phone back in his pocket. "Who was that?" I asked, but of course, he ignored my question and kept walking. "So you're not going to tell me anything about what's going on?" I pressed, trying to get some sort of response from him. Still nothing. He was really starting to aggravate me. He'd said I needed to tell him everything for my safety, but somehow the same rules didn't apply to him? "Can you at least tell me what we're doing, or where we're going?" I asked, but still I didn't get a response. After another block walked in strained silence, I stopped dead in my tracks. It took him a second to realize I was no longer walking, but once he did, it was clear he was pissed.

"What the hell are you doing?" he hissed, quickly closing the distance between us. "Stop acting like a child. Let's go."

I squared my shoulders, defiantly staring up at him. "No, not until you tell me what the hell we're doing. This is ridiculous! I have no clue what's going on, and you won't answer me or tell me anything!"

"This is not the time or place to discuss this," he replied, but I didn't falter. I held my ground, never breaking eye contact with him. After he realized I wasn't budging, he let out a loud, frustrated sigh, "Okay, listen… please follow me for another few blocks. We'll grab a cab, and I'll tell you where we're going, okay?"

"And you'll tell me who that was on the phone and what the conversation was about?" I asked, watching him run his hands roughly over the stubble on his chin.

"Don't press your luck. Now come on," he answered before taking off again. It wasn't exactly the response I was looking for, but it was better than nothing. I followed him as we quickly headed onto a busy block with an abundance of cabs driving around. He hailed one, and we climbed in. "Oak Hill Cemetery, please."

I froze. Why the hell were we going to a cemetery? Especially with everything that had been going on – it seemed incredibly ominous.

"Um… I'm not sure I'm comfortable with going to—" I began in a whisper, but he quickly cut me off.

"I know cemeteries are a little unconventional for sightseeing, but this place is beautiful. Besides, the area is one of the oldest and most prestigious in the city. There are lots of other interesting venues near there that we'll be able to check out while we're here. We won't stay long, but I think it's worth seeing. Trust me, darling," Kane answered affectionately, kissing the palm of my hand as if we were a couple. What the hell was going on?

Judging from the smug smile he gave me, he was amused by the stunned expression I was currently wearing. He was obviously telling me something with his cryptic little message, something that had little to do with the cemetery, but I couldn't focus with him kissing my palms and rubbing his thumb affectionately on my forearm. After a lot of effort on my part, forcing myself to ignore his touch and his close proximity, it dawned on me. He'd mentioned 'lots of other interesting venues near there'. James lived in the area. Of course! This was annoyingly cryptic, but obviously Kane's way of trying to cover our tracks in case this driver was ever questioned. "I'm sorry, I'm not trying to scare you or make you uncomfortable. I know I can be a little pushy, but I don't mean to be. I'm just used to people following my orders without complaint or question," he whispered, giving me a weak smile.

"It's fine, I trust you," I answered honestly, grabbing his hand in mine, and offering him a small smile in return. I meant it, too. No matter what happened between Kane and me, there was something about him I trusted wholeheartedly. Our eyes met, and I could see the confusion lingering in his. He kissed my palm again, sending all kinds of crazy wonderful sensations cascading through my body. He infuriated me, and yet a simple, fake kiss to my palm could send every one of my nerve endings into a fevered reaction. For better or worse, it was clear I was still attracted to Kane, and as much as it angered me to feel that way, my body had made the decision for me. It was also clear I was still alive because of him, so I decided that although I didn't always have to like him, like a good soldier I would follow my commander anywhere. It was obviously what he was used to and what he needed from me, so it was the least I could do to make things easier on him. Hopefully, we could figure this out without killing each other or getting killed. I prayed we could save James, too.

Kane

I was relieved when Kendall quickly understood why I wanted to go to the cemetery. I have to admit, it surprised me a little when she took hold of my hand. I wished it hadn't felt so comfortable when she did it. I needed to focus on the task at hand.

The cemetery worked out as planned. We spent a little time touring the gravestones, before exiting and making our way through side streets to James' place. Once we arrived at his property, I spent some time surveying the area. The fact that his house wasn't swarming with police officers told me that those charming individuals we'd seen in action last night had done a good job of covering everything up. James was an important public figure, so it wouldn't take long for people to start asking questions and wondering where he was. I went into the groundskeeper's shed and found a can of spray paint.

"What's that for?"

"Stay back for a minute. I'm going to spray the camera. You can head to the door once I do that," I offered, making my way over to the hidden camera. I stretched my arm up and sprayed the device. Seeing my nod, Kendall rushed over to the door and stood in front of it, glancing around anxiously. "Please unlock the door," I said, wondering why she hadn't already done so.

"Why would I be able to unlock the door? I don't have the code," she stated, furrowing her brow in confusion.

"Oh, no reason. I just thought you'd know it," I responded, a little surprised. I guess this meant their relationship wasn't on a 'key to the front door' level. Luckily for us, I did happen to have the code. It was a stroke of pure luck that James had given it to me, in a desperate attempt to convince me to stay with him. I retrieved it from my wallet and punched in the numbers. We stepped inside, and I took out my RF pen to begin scanning for any bugged devices.

"What the hell is that?" she questioned, following close behind. She was so close I could smell her apple and pear scented shampoo. Suddenly, I was ripped back into a memory of the other night, and our embrace. I could remember the sensation of her body pressed close to mine. I zoned back into the present, a little surprised at how much a scent could affect the body.

"It's a transmitter scanner," I answered, taking a few large steps to try and create some distance between us.

"Surveillance stuff? Did you use that at my place too?" she asked, keeping her voice at a whisper.

"Yeah, I did. It's not the most powerful scanner available, but it does the job, and it happens to be a pen, too, which can come in handy." I smiled, and Kendall smiled back. Someone in my command had given them as joke gifts one Christmas when we were on a mission, but they'd ended up being beneficial; discreet, easy to carry and useful when you wanted to do a quick scan. It didn't pick up any transmitters in James' place, which meant whoever was orchestrating this kidnapping didn't think anyone would come here. It was clear however, that someone had been here and gone through the place. There could only be one of two options: the first was that they'd found what they were looking for, or the second – they were satisfied it wasn't here. They'd done a decent job of covering their tracks, but they weren't perfect. Had it not been for the one misplaced ornament on James' mantle, and the slightly crooked picture frame above it, his otherwise O.C.D. level of organization looked untouched.

"Someone was definitely here," I told Kendall as she looked around apprehensively. "I wish I had some sort of idea what they were looking for. As a precaution, try not to touch anything directly."

She nodded and walked over to the living room, putting her bag down beside the couch. "Should we turn on the TV?" she asked, grabbing the TV remote with her sleeve.

"What for?"

"I want to see if they have any kind of report on James or Dom," she explained, sounding a little unsure.

"That's a good idea," I replied, and saw a relieved smile spread across her lips as she turned on the television to a local newscast. I hadn't been giving her enough credit, because she had some really good ideas and was quite impressive at offering valid suggestions I hadn't necessarily thought about. I turned my attention to James' bookshelf, rifling through his books. It's always hard to know where to start looking for something, when you have no idea what it is. It didn't help that I knew so little about James that I couldn't even begin to know where nhe might hide something.

"Oh my God! Oh my God!" Kendall repeated, sounding horror-stricken.

I spotted a breaking news story which flashed pictures of three women across the screen. "Three women were found dead early this morning at the sight of a single vehicle accident. Moira Nickson, Lindsay Martin and Casey Peters have been identified as the victims of this tragic accident. They died when their small black 2014 Mercedes-Benz CLA 250 crashed into a tree located on St. Augustine's middle school property, creating a rather gruesome scene. The official cause of the accident is not currently known, and no further details have been provided at this time. School has been canceled at St. Augustine's for the day, in order to assist officials in their investigation and clean up. We will continue to report developments as they become available."

"Did you know any of them?" I asked, walking over to her as she perched on the couch, covering her mouth with her hands. "Kendall…" I said softly, crouching down to face her, "did you know them?"

She nodded, her skin pale. "Yes, I knew all of them. They worked for Dom. Oh my God, Kane! They probably killed them! It would be a huge coincidence that three of my coworkers died on the same night as all this happened and it not be related. They killed all of them and made it look like an accident! They're going to kill me, aren't they?"

My heart broke as her panic-stricken eyes bore into mine. These women had to have something to do with James. This was clearly bigger than I'd imagined. Whoever these kidnappers were, they were taking out anyone involved. I had to figure out what was going on before they tried to hurt Kendall. I needed to find out what the hell this was about; it would be too hard to protect her otherwise. There were still too many questions and too much uncertainty. "No, they won't. I won't let that happen. I promised you that I would keep you safe, and I intend to see that through," I assured her, meaning every word. I pulled her into my arms, holding her tightly. She seemed so frightened and fragile right now, and I couldn't help feeling angry and protective over her. A few minutes passed and I realized I was still hugging her, so I slowly let go. I got up and put some distance between us. I would do whatever I could to keep her safe, even if that meant keeping her safe from me. For the moment, I had a job to do. "Do you know of any reason why they would have killed them? I can't make sense of what's going on, but obviously it has something to do with James."

"No, I can't," she offered. "I've been trying to figure out what the hell James did or what he was involved in, but I can't think of a thing. All I know is that whatever the hell he and Dominique were up to, it royally screwed us all, by association," she replied, sounding as exasperated as I felt. People were being killed; James had been kidnapped; this whole thing was a mess, but I felt certain Kendall would tell me if she thought of anything that could help. But I still didn't understand why they wanted her, if she knew nothing. One of the puzzle pieces was missing, and whether she realized it or not, Kendall either knew something without being aware of it, or they thought she did. If she did in fact, know nothing, it would make no difference to them, but it would make it a lot more difficult to figure this out.

"Did any of those women know where you live?"

"No, we didn't hang out, outside of events. One of Dominique's rules was that we don't socialize outside of work and exchange personal information. Some people didn't take the rule seriously, but I did. I liked the separation between my two lives. No one had my real address, name or personal cell phone number."

"What about James?"

"What about James?" she asked, sounding confused by the question.

"Did he talk to those girls that you know of? Did he know where you lived? Did he have your personal number, so they might be able to find it on his phone?" I asked hesitantly, not really wanting to hear her response. I wasn't sure how close she and James were, but I definitely didn't want to hear details about it.

She narrowed her eyes. "What are you asking? What is it that you think James and I were, exactly? Do you think I'm his girlfriend, or maybe his personal fucking concubine?" She spat the words angrily, surprising me. "Let's get one thing straight about James and me. We only had sex a handful of times, over seven years ago. That was before I even started in this escort shit. I love James as a friend; I owe him a lot, but I am not his personal whore or his girlfriend!

And given that you know so little about your brother, but like to think nothing but the worst about him and anyone he associates with, let me enlighten you, Kane. He and Dominique had a very unique relationship, and she wouldn't have taken kindly to him screwing all her girls. He took her girls to events as dates from time to time and liked taking me because we were friends. Not to mention that I was very good at my job, which I don't expect you to understand, but it's the truth! I guess that because he took me out so much, it might have given people the wrong impression about us being in a relationship, and truthfully he liked them thinking that way. It gave him a reason to leave events early and get away from the ridiculous people in his world, most of whom he despised. So to answer your questions, no, he wasn't the type to bring women here that I know of, but I wasn't his keeper, so I don't know for sure. I can't answer whether he had their contact information either, but I can't see why he would," she stated, her eyes burning with anger. "Now what was the point of that question?"

"I was just wondering if whoever killed those women could have found them through James, somehow. I don't think it's a coincidence that they died on the same night this happened, and I know this is all linked somehow, but… I don't understand what this it's all about because right now, I just can't make sense of it," I answered, my thoughts and emotions a little overloaded from the ton of information she'd just thrown at me. One part of me was livid that she was giving me shit for judging my brother and for knowing nothing about him. She had no right to comment on our relationship, or lack thereof. Moreover, no matter how relieved I felt that she and James hadn't been 'together' in a long time, I still didn't understand the ins and outs of their relationship, or their history together, which seemed to be very complex. I wasn't trying to hurt her, but I wasn't used to dealing with matters which had this many emotions involved. Things were so much easier when you didn't have a bunch of feelings in the mix, causing additional confusion.

"Fine," she answered simply, still looking aggravated. Regardless of my feelings about her or my brother, I needed to get my head on straight. My life was turning into a fucking soap opera, which was not helpful given all I was trying to deal with. "I'm going to do some cyber research on his computer. Let me know if you find anything in the house that I should see," I stated, walking over to her backpack and retrieving her laptop. I sat down at the kitchen island and started hacking my way onto an external proxy, to snoop through James' computer data. My plan was to grab everything I could off his computer's hard drive, so I could dig through it later. I had to try and get access using a back door, in case someone had put an alert on his computer after they did their own digging. I noticed a ton of data had been deleted, which I gathered was the stuff that might be worth looking at. Whoever had gotten rid of it hadn't done the best job, and I hoped whoever was here before me wasn't as good at finding stuff as I was.

"What are you doing?" Kendall asked curiously, standing behind me and watching my every move from over my shoulder.

"I'm trying to access James' deleted files. Someone erased a lot of data, but I think I can get it back."

"So you're hacking?"

"Yeah."

"So you're a hacker?"

"Well, if the fact that I can hack makes me a hacker, then yes, I'm a hacker," I answered smugly.

She released an irritated sigh. "Let me guess, you learned this particular skill-set as part of your career in the SEALs," she announced in an equally smug tone. The word 'SEALs' caused my heart rate to spike. How did she know I was a part of the SEALs? I'd told her I was military, but I never specified who I worked for. It isn't like I'm not allowed to tell anyone about my profession, I just can't talk about any specifics. The problem was that people always wanted specifics. Besides, I wasn't sure I trusted her enough to give her any more details about my life. Still, she was incredibly perceptive because I doubted that James would have told her. He knew that I wouldn't appreciate him giving details about my life to anyone. We might not have known each other very well on a personal level, but we both knew about each other's careers and the importance of keeping secrets about them.

"I don't know where you're getting your information from, but I learned this skill at school," I answered, without addressing the SEALs comment. Besides, I wasn't exactly lying–I had learned my computer skills in school. Granted, it was while getting my degrees in Computer Science and Cyber Operations from the Naval Academy and from on-the-job training, but still, she didn't need to know that.

"Oh, so a Naval Intelligence Officer of sorts I see, very interesting," she replied, trying to get more information out of me. I refused to engage any further on the topic. It was the best way to stop encouraging her questions. It didn't take long for her to lose interest, and she eventually stepped away from me while I kept searching James' deleted history. There was a lot of information about secret meetings with a lobbyist and other individuals, but nothing that would be important enough to kill for. A series of encrypted files caught my attention, and they turned out to contain date and time stamps along with what looked like locations. There were also two sets of letters which appeared to be initials, beside some sort of encoded descriptor. I didn't have time to try and decipher what all this meant, so I decided to take them with me. It was probably time to head out.

I shut down the computer and stuffed it back into Kendall's backpack. I looked around, but couldn't see Kendall anywhere. "Kendall," I called out, but she didn't answer. I walked up the stairs leading to the second floor, "Kendall?" I called again, but still got no answer.

Panic shot through me. What if I hadn't checked the premises thoroughly enough, and someone had stayed behind? I ran down the hall, checking each room until I heard movement in the master bedroom. I quietly approached the closet, ready to take down whoever might be in there but all I found was Kendall, rummaging through boxes in James' closet.

"What are you doing?" I asked, both relieved and irritated. This woman really had a way of getting under my skin.

She tilted her head and offered me a sarcastic smile. "I'm knitting a sweater," she announced, making a smile creep onto my lips.

She giggled before returning her attention to the boxes she'd placed on the floor. "I haven't found anything of interest yet, but James was smart enough not to keep incriminating documents in the open," she offered, still deep in thought.

"We should really get going soon."

"Yeah, I know. I just can't help thinking there's something here," she said, shaking her head in frustration. "Where are we going anyway?"

"Listen, I have a hotel room. No one knows where it is. I got James' limo driver to pick me up at a coffee shop, a few blocks from my hotel," I stated. Her eyebrows shot up, clearly perplexed. "What?" I laughed. "You're wondering why I didn't get picked up at my hotel?"

She nodded. "I didn't want James to know where I was staying, because I didn't want him to show up there and try to push me into seeing him if last night didn't go well," I answered, watching her eyes soften with understanding. "Anyway," I said, bringing us back to the topic at hand, "I think it will be safe to go there, at least for tonight."

She got up and walked over to one of the custom-built dressers. Opening one of the drawers, she reached in and pulled out a blue sweater, handing it to me.

"What's this for?" I asked.

"You still have a little blood visible on your dress shirt. If nothing else, you and James are about the same shirt size." She laughed uncomfortably.

I scoffed aloud; I personally thought I was in way better shape than he was. "Thanks," I said, unbuttoning my dress shirt and seeing a blush settle on her cheeks as she averted her eyes. I found it ironic that this small gesture made her so uncomfortable, given her former profession. "Okay, we should go," I offered, once I had the sweater on. It actually did fit perfectly.

"Yeah, I know," she replied, sounding uncertain, suddenly fidgeting impatiently.

"What's wrong?"

"I just feel like there's something here that we're missing," she said, running her hands through her newly-cut hair.

"Did James ever mention a special place where he liked to keep things?"

"No, not really, but…" Her voice trailed off as she fixated on the area rug on the floor. "Please, help me move this," she asked suddenly as she crouched down to tug at it. I walked over and yanked up the rug, finding nothing but hardwood.

"You look disappointed," I said when she bit her lip nervously.

"I could have sworn I saw him pull something out of a spot around here before…" she began, hooking her finger into a small, hollow knot in the wood. She pulled up, exposing what appeared to be a hidden trap door with a safe contained within it.

"Holy shit!" I exclaimed, my smile matching hers. She'd been right about something being here, and thankfully, she hadn't given up on looking for it.

"I remembered seeing him grab something from his closet floor. It was years ago, but I still remembered it."

We both stared at the safe. "Do you know the code?" I asked, quickly realizing from her fading smile that she didn't.

"No, I don't! Dammit! I don't even think James knows that I saw him go into this." She huffed in frustration, running her fingers through her hair.

"We're screwed. I can't even begin to guess what the code could be." I sighed audibly, rubbing my face. "We don't have time to start cutting into this thing, either." We'd finally appeared to catch a break and we were still miles away from being able to sort out what it was.

She sat wordlessly, deep in thought, before she looked up at me. I knew that look — she had an idea, but seemed uncertain about saying it aloud. "What's up Kendall?"

"I have an idea, but I'm worried that if I'm wrong, the safe might seize up or something, and we won't get another shot."

"I say let's try it. We have nothing to lose."

She nodded. "Okay then. What's your date of birth?"

"My date of birth?" I repeated, not sure I'd heard the question correctly.

"What's your birthday, Kane? Tell it to me numerically," she requested. "Come on, we don't have all day," she added impatiently.

"010680," I offered, watching her input my birth date into the keypad. "I really don't think he would use my—" I began, but the beep that followed stunned me into silence. My brother – a man who I thought had abandoned and forgotten all about me – had used my birth date as the combination to his hidden safe. Each time he opened this safe, he thought of me. I felt an odd tightening in my chest.

Kendall's eyes widened in surprise, "Holy shit! I didn't actually think that would work," she whispered, staring down at the open safe which contained a large stack of folders and cash.

I regained my composure, remembering the severity of our situation. We didn't have time to hang around. "Grab the folders and leave the cash. Then we'll put everything back to where it was. We have to go."

Chapter 10

Kendall

Sitting in Kane's hotel room, I was suddenly hit full force with the realization of what had occurred over the last few days. Everything about my life was totally chaotic right now, people were trying to kill me, and people I knew were dying. James was still gone, and my feelings for Kane were all over the place. Not to mention the fact that his own feelings about James were all over the place, which happened to be an additional complication. I couldn't help feeling both emotionally and physically exhausted, and the thought of spending the night here with Kane had me all kinds of stressed-out. I knew it didn't matter, because he made it clear he wasn't interested in me due to my former profession and my history with James, but that didn't change the fact my body was incredibly attracted to him. This attraction overthrew any rational reasoning I had and made me temporarily forget all about his asshole tendencies. I knew that was sad on so many levels, as I was a strong and independent woman with self-respect, but dammit, sometimes the vagina wins out, whether you like it or not.

I sat down on the couch of his modest suite, not really sure what to do with myself. "Do you want something to eat?" he asked, waving casually at the phone. "I can order some room service."

"No, that's okay... Truthfully, I'm not really that hungry right now. I'll just order a pizza later or something... if that's okay," I answered awkwardly, seeing him nod as he walked over to a duffel bag on the floor near the bed. He pulled out a few pieces of clothing and headed into the bathroom.

Seeing the door close, I exhaled with relief that he hadn't just changed in front of me. I couldn't help gawking at him like an idiot, and I really didn't need to deal with that right now. He reappeared a few minutes later, dressed in a great pair of dark wash jeans and fitted black sweater with the sleeves pushed up at his forearms. I don't know how he made something so basic look so good, and I practically had to wipe the drool from my face when he approached. "Okay, Kendall, I'm going to run out and meet someone. Don't leave. Don't call anyone. Don't go online. Don't answer the phone or the door. In fact, don't do anything. I'll order pizza or whatever when I get back. I won't be long."

I remembered he had spoken to someone earlier and said he would meet them L. Memorial. I wished he would tell me who this mystery person was, so I didn't feel so out of the loop. But I knew he wouldn't tell me, even if I asked, so I just nodded my agreement. He grabbed his keys from the coffee table and left the hotel room, which suddenly seemed incredibly quiet. I found myself feeling a little vulnerable. I doubt he would have left me here alone if he thought I was at risk, and he'd said he wouldn't let anything happen to me, but I couldn't help being nervous.

I decided I needed to shake it off and keep my mind busy, so I grabbed one of the folders we'd found in James' safe. All I could control was the here and now, so the least I could was make myself useful and see what I could find in these folders. I opened the first one and began scrutinizing every last detail of each page. If there is something in any of these, I vowed to find it.

※

Kane

Thankfully, Jeremy was able to meet me on such short notice. To ensure our safety, I made sure to get to the meeting site early, to make sure no one was following either of us. I've known Jeremy a long time, and I trust him. He had always been the type of guy I could count on. We enlisted in the Navy the same month and attended the Naval Academy together. Eventually, we worked to-gether as Naval Intelligence Officers. Our lives took different paths after that, though. I decided to become a Navy SEAL and he stayed in Intel, but we've stayed in touch ever since. If anyone could give me some dirt on my brother, it would be Jeremy. I would have to be careful. The last thing I wanted was to en-danger Jeremy; especially since I couldn't be certain how deep this conspiracy went. Dirty cops might only be the tip of the iceberg. But if I wanted to get to the bottom of this, I couldn't play it too safe. "Well, well, well, if it isn't Senior Chief Clarke, or should I say, the future Master Chief Kane Clarke. Ladies and Gentlemen, brace yourselves for the presence of greatness," Jeremy joked as he approached me, his hand extended to mine for a friendly handshake.

"Yeah, keep it down. I'd hate to disappoint when I'm forced to retire as a senior chief," I laughed too, pulling him in for a hug. "Besides, haven't you heard? I'm damaged goods. I'm on 'recommended' leave."

"Yeah, I heard, but after what happened I don't blame you for needing some time. Actually, I'm more surprised this is your first leave," he offered sympa-thetically running his thumb and index fingers along his strong chin. "Not that I want to get into a whole thing here, but how are you doing? I'm not going to lie; you look like shit."

"I'm fine," I offered weakly watching his brow crease skeptically, "Seriously, never mind me, how are you doing? How are Sheryl and the kids?" I asked, changing the subject. With everything going on, the last thing I wanted to do was talk about my reasons for not being at work.

"Everyone is good. Sheryl is, well… she's Sheryl and that means she's an argumentatively bossy woman who is currently hooked on spinning classes. The kids are great. You should come by and see them, they're getting big and starting school soon. So overall, it's wonderful chaos." He laughed, his smile causing the dark skin at the corner of his black eyes to crinkle. "But I know you, Kane, you didn't call me to catch-up. Why don't you tell me what you really need? Don't get me wrong, it's not that I don't enjoy getting a random call from you to meet up all secret and shit, but my guess is you have other things you want to talk about. So let's get to that."

"All right," I offered, as he rolled his wrist in a circular motion with his right index finger extended, telling me to get on it. "Have you heard any rumblings or rumors about someone having it in for my brother?"

"Your brother is a major power player, so he's bound to have an enemy or two somewhere, but all anyone is talking about today is how three of Dominique's girls were found dead in some kind of car accident. People are anxious to get your brother's thoughts on it, given how close he and Dominique are."

"You know about Dominique and my brother?" I asked, a little surprised by how far out of the political loop I'd been, prior to all this. I'd heard Dominique was a madam, and I'd assumed she was my brothers' keeper or whatever when he was in the game, but I didn't know anything about how close they'd remained afterwards.

"Of course I do. Everyone does. Dominique is the top escort provider for the suits and figureheads in the entire city. She's successful because she knows the right people, pays the right people, and she's the most discreet, which is why she's been in the business for so long. From what I understand, your brother is not only a customer, but a close friend of hers. A few people in our inner circle have used her services from time to time, and it didn't take long for the connection to be made with the three dead women."

"So people aren't buying the whole 'accident' angle that's being reported?" I asked apprehensively. If people were connecting the dots, it would only be a matter of time until they found Dominique and then started searching for James. In my experience, this meant they would be increasing their efforts to find Kendall, and my worry was that if James was still alive, his time was swiftly running out.

"No one who knows that they worked for Dominique is buying that story. Those women were apparently at some important party that night and left in a hurry. It doesn't help that there are conflicting reports about some damage to the rear of the vehicle, which wouldn't make sense if they lost control and slammed into a tree."

"Can I ask you do a little digging for me? I really need to find out anything that could have gotten my brother into hot water. Anything you can dig up would be helpful," I requested, and saw a perplexed expression settle on his face.

"What's going on, Kane?" he asked, folding his arms over his chest. "I know you well enough to know when you're being purposely cryptic."

"Listen, I know. I hate to ask you, but right now I don't even know what puzzle pieces to put together, to even try and explain what's going on. Can you help?"

"Yeah, of course. I don't really know what you're looking for, but I'll see what I can dig up. How soon do you need this?" he asked, running his fingers through his short, black hair.

"Fast... like, tonight fast... Say 2200hours?" I requested. I knew it wasn't giving him much time to do research, but in our business, we've done things on shorter time frames.

"Yeah... sure. I don't know what I'll find, but I'll let you know."

"Thank you, Jeremy. Text my cell for a meeting spot... And, Jeremy; I hate to even mention this but—"

"Yeah, yeah, I know. I'll be discreet," he said, cutting me off. "This isn't my first rodeo," he joked, a hint of his thick southern accent seeping through into his otherwise usually controlled speech. I nodded, and we headed in opposite directions.

To be safe, I made sure to take the long way back to the hotel, making sure I weaved through any back alleys and side streets I could until I was satisfied that no one was behind me. I suspected things were about to get very interesting, very fast.

Kendall

My heart fluttered when I heard the door's keyless lock beep. Kane was back. He entered the suite's living room and his jaw practically hit the ground, "What the hell are you doing?" he asked, flabbergasted, as he scanned the floor. The entire room was covered in fanned out pages from James' folders.

"I got bored and felt a little useless, so I decided to make myself useful," I offered casually, trying very hard to not notice how good he looked.

"Okay…" he offered calmly, although his jaw was clenched when he sat down on the couch beside me. "So, other than showing me how much of a mess you can make, what have you've found out?"

He was clearly annoyed and possibly a little skeptical about my abilities, but nonetheless I appreciated that he was giving me the benefit of the doubt, even if he was sort of rude about it. "Okay, this might look like chaos, but I assure you it's organized chaos," I announced confidently, picking up the furthest pile of documents to my left and handing them to him. "Each pile represents a different incriminating and criminal act, such as adultery and drugs possession," I stated as he examined the documents. I grabbed another pile. "This group outlines those with charges listed involving bribery and tax fraud."

"Okay, so this is a collection of files recording criminal acts or at the very least, questionable behavior? So what? Who are they for? What's the connection? Why the hell would James be collecting a bunch of documents like this?" he questioned thoughtfully. "This seems so random."

"You're right. They do appear to be random, comprising hundreds of different wrongdoings, but I noticed certain reports, such as those concerning wire fraud, conspiracy, extortion, sexual assault, racketeering, money laundering and bribery, have hand-drawn stars on the corner of the page." I watched as he quickly flipped through the sheets, finding some of the pages with the stars.

"The other thing I noticed, was what appears to be hand-written initials on each page, which is what I used to sort them into groups. There are multiples of the same initials, and some pages have more than one set of initials. In total, I've found twenty different sets of initials."

He nodded, flipping through a new pile. "Yeah, that's right, there are. I see them. Any idea whose initials they are?"

"No," I answered, running my hands through my hair. "I haven't gotten that far yet. Sorry."

"Sorry?" he said, his beautiful brown eyes fixed on me. "You have nothing to be sorry about. You did great. This is very helpful."

My cheeks heated under his steady gaze. "Thanks," I replied. I noticed that his eyes suddenly seemed to be scanning every inch of me. The heat of the blush grew.

He cleared his throat before swiftly replacing the pages into tidy stacks on the floor, "Listen, you should take a break," he stated. 'Why don't you go take a bath or a shower, and I'll order that pizza we talked about earlier."

"Yes, I could use a break. Pizza would be great," I answered, getting up from the floor just as he rose from his crouched position. I tried to move past his towering frame, but I was sandwiched between the couch and the coffee table, causing us to both do that really awkward, 'trying to pass each other' thing. Eventually, Kane stepped around me as I quickly gathered my things and headed into the bathroom, closing the door behind me. I stood with my back against the door, trying to calm my rapid breathing and pounding heartbeat. I wished that Kane and I hadn't met before all this madness began. At least that way I wouldn't be so distracted by him. I certainly wouldn't have to know how good a kisser he was, and how amazing it felt when he touched me. I walked over to the bathtub and turned the knobs, deciding to opt for a cold shower.

Chapter 11

Kane

After I'd ordered the pizza, I poured myself a glass of whiskey, courtesy of the room's mini-bar. I wasn't exactly thrilled at paying ten dollars for an ounce of booze, but I needed something to take the edge off because I'd found myself pacing the room, unable to sit still. I couldn't seem to stop thinking about the fact that Kendall was naked and showering in the room next door. This knowledge had an arousing effect my body. Given everything going on, I wished sex wasn't on my mind, but let's face it — it was nearly impossible to be around Kendall and *not* think about it. My mind might still be working through everything, and I wasn't sure how I felt about her, but my libido clearly didn't have the same reservations. My libido apparently liked Kendall just fine and wanted nothing more than for me to be inside her.

I wished she could be annoying or idiotic, because at least then I could find something to dislike about her, but she wasn't. She was far from it; in fact, she was bright, kind and strong. She'd kept up with me every step of the way, through all the chaos, without complaint. Those were all things that only made her sexier, and I found myself more attracted to her the more time we spent together.

I heard the bathroom door open, and Kendall walked out. Her hair was dripping water onto the tight white tank top she wore. "Fuck," I hissed under my breath, my cock hardening at the sight. I needed to get a grip because this was ridiculous. I just prayed she couldn't tell how my body was reacting around her. She bent over to retrieve a hair tie from her bag, and it was all over for me. I had to get the hell out of there, immediately.

I slammed down the rest of my drink. "I'm going to go wait for the pizza in the lobby. Be right back," I said abruptly, heading out the door without saying another word. I stalked down the hall, my jeans tight, feeling like a total tool. I was a grown-ass man, acting like a fucking teenager with no self-control. I'd been relieved we hadn't slept together the other night, but now I couldn't help but wonder if it wouldn't have been better to get her out of my system. Even as the thought crossed my mind, something told me she wouldn't be the type of woman you could ever really get out of your system, especially after getting a taste.

I got to the lobby just in time to grab the pizza. I paid the guy and slowly made my way back up to the room, thankfully giving me enough time to calm my body down before seeing her again. There were plenty of other, far more important things to think about, and yet they were all shot straight to hell when I saw her smile as I entered the hotel room.

"You're my hero! I'm so hungry!" she said, following me to the table where I set the pizza box down.

I laughed watching her devour two slices within minutes. "Wow, you really are hungry."

"Yeah, I am," she laughed. "And I bet you are too. I don't think you even ate today."

I hadn't eaten, but I hadn't really thought about it until now. There were many days while on missions when I'd gone without a proper meal. "No I guess I haven't."

"You're probably trained to push past hunger though, right? Like a sort of survival skill? I imagine some of the places you go for missions don't have food readily available," she commented, her eyebrow arched in anticipation of my response.

For whatever reason, probably curiosity, I was feeling inclined to oblige her prying. "You think you have me all figured out, don't you?"

"I've already told you what I've figured out. Navy SEALs, where you're clearly involved with computers, given your ninja cyber skills. I think you're probably a highly ranked officer, because I know you've been doing this since you were eighteen and, well, you seem good at it," she stated confidently, taking a bite of her pizza slice.

I was actually pretty impressed by how much she'd managed to pick up about me without me saying anything. She was bang on, but I still wasn't going to let her know that. "You have a vivid imagination, Kendall," I offered simply.

"Tell me I'm wrong. Look me in the face and tell me I'm way off, and I won't bring it up again," she insisted, her eyes intensely focused on mine. I found myself tongue-tied beneath her gaze. For whatever reason, I couldn't spit out the denial required to convince her. I was usually good at convincing people about pretty much anything, but right then I couldn't. This woman has rendered me speechless. "That's what I thought," she answered, a smug smile spreading on her lips.

My phone buzzed, announcing a text message from Jeremy. Got something, I read, my pulse quickening slightly. I quickly texted him back. 2200? Still ok? I questioned, knowing tomorrow would be an pivotal day in this situation. It had been forty-eight hours since these events had started to unfold, and everything was starting to unravel. The kidnappers would be trying to tie up any loose ends, which included getting rid of James and Kendall. I needed answers and I needed them very soon. Sounds good. Meet me at The Loft, Jeremy texted back.

I glanced at the clock on the bedside table, confirming we still had an hour before I had to meet him. The Loft was a hotel bar, about four blocks from my hotel. It was a good-sized venue, providing enough clientele so we could blend in for some privacy. It was also close enough that we could easily make a run for it, if needed.

"Everything okay?" Kendall questioned, eyeing me curiously.

"Yeah, I have to meet a friend nearby at ten," I stated, taking a large bite from my slice of pizza.

"Can I come with you?"

"No, I think you should stay here." I didn't want to have to worry about her at every turn.

"No, please, hear me out? I'll go incognito; I'll wear a hat and a baggy sweater. People will think I'm a guy," she offered, nodding her head enthusiastically as though this would somehow convince me.

"Give me a break, Kendall; you couldn't look like a guy if you tried."

"I can be whatever you need me to be, just please don't leave me again. I'll go crazy sitting here worrying about everything. I feel safer when I'm with you," she stated, her voice edging on the point of desperation. A part of me knew it was a bad idea, but I couldn't handle that look on her face. I nodded reluctantly, cursing myself internally as I did it. Relief washed over her expression. At least this way I could keep an eye on what she was doing. That's what I told myself, anyway.

"Kendall... you have to do everything I say, okay? If I say be quiet, I expect you to be quiet and if I say run, you run. Got it?"

"I know, Kane. Thank you for letting me come with you. How long do we have before we need to leave?" she asked, walking over to her bag and pulling out a flat iron.

"About forty-five minutes," I stated, watching her movements. "You packed that?" I asked, dumbfounded that this was one of the items she'd deemed essential.

"Of course I did. I need this," she stated matter-of-factly, as though I'd asked a completely ridiculous question. She grimaced as I rolled my eyes in disbelief. "Oh, you just worry about your own stuff!"

In fact, I was suddenly aware of how very little I knew about women. I'd never really had to share space with one before for this length of time, and it was odd being in such close quarters with the opposite sex.

"I meant to ask you," she called out, walking toward the bathroom. "Did you find anything on James' computer?" I wasn't sure if it was the sleep deprivation or the more, ah... primal urges that had me so distracted, but I'd forgotten all about the data I'd collected on his computer. "I was just wondering if you found anything that might explain any of those initials."

Holy shit, this woman was a genius! I *had* found files on James' computer that contained initials, locations and time stamps, along with some encrypted data. I'd bet money they matched the ones on papers Kendall had all over the floor. I ran over and grabbed her computer, opening up the stored folders I'd retrieved from James' computer. I compared the initials on the sheets of paper to the different electronic folders and sure enough – they matched.

"Well?" she asked after several minutes, walking towards me with freshly-straightened hair, "Anything?"

"I think so. See these files here," I offered, pointing them out to her. "The initials appear to match the ones on the documents. I still don't know who the initials belong to, but we now know that the documents are linked. We have time and location stamps. Additionally, I also noticed this second set of initials on the bottom corner of the electronic pages."

She furrowed her brows as she scrutinized the initials. I watched the color drain from her face. "I think I know those initials."

"Really?"

"Even though I didn't know them by their real names until this morning; M.N. is Moira Nickson, L.M. is Lindsay Martin and C.P. is Casey Peters," she said, swallowing hard.

"The dead escorts?" I questioned, and she nodded in response. We'd been right all along; they did die because of something to do with James, and this was the proof. Whoever was behind this had killed them because of it.

I glanced at the clock on the nightstand, confirming it was time to leave. I shut the computer and placed it down on the coffee table. Kendall seemed a little shaken by all this and was sitting on the arm of the chair, chewing at her nail anxiously. "Kendall are you all right?"

"I'm okay, or at least, I will be," she answered in a small voice, her eyes meeting mine. I found myself mesmerized by them – they reminded me of an intense storm – profound, powerful and unpredictable, while all the while being terrifyingly beautiful. Abruptly, it felt as if I'd been swept up in an electric current. I was overcome with the urge to kiss her. I tried to push it back down, but my body almost ached with the need. I watched Kendall's breathing increase and knew she was experiencing the same thing. There was something between us, and we were like two magnets being drawn together, our bodies growing more charged with every passing second. I broke first, overcome with the need to touch her, and no matter how loudly my head protested, I couldn't stop myself. I reached over and pulled her to me, our lips locking into a passionate kiss. She ran her fingers through my hair as our bodies began moving against each other, trying to get as close to one another as we could. Her kiss intensified, and my body kicked into overdrive. I suddenly found myself experiencing a jumble of confused feelings. Thoughts of James came rushing into my mind and I was torn between anger and hurt, all the while battling my primal desire to touch every part of Kendall. I wanted to know all of her.

In that instant I knew I would do anything to protect her. I'd give up my life for this woman, which I knew was madness, but it was the truth. I wasn't sure if it was merely lust or something much more powerful, but whatever it was, it was the most intense feeling I'd ever experienced. My phone vibrated in my jeans pocket, snapping me back to reality. What the hell was I doing? This was insane; we shouldn't be doing this right now. We didn't need the additional complication, and besides, Jeremy was waiting for us.

"We can't do this. We should go," I breathed, pulling away from her, severing the electric connection we'd been lost in a moment ago. She closed her beautiful, lust-filled eyes, running her fingers through her hair and breathing fast and hard. She nodded, walking over to grab her jacket. I followed suit and grabbed my own. When I turned back and faced her, I felt like a complete asshole when I noticed the hurt expression on her face.

Kendall

I followed Kane to our destination, and found myself growing angrier with every step. How could I be so stupid? How could I give up my control to him so easily? I'd completely lost myself in that hotel room, which should never have happened. I knew better. I might not be an escort anymore, but the skills I'd learned were transferable. The rules were the same–don't let anyone seduce you. No matter how much he liked to pretend he didn't, Kane wanted me. But wanting me wasn't enough. Plenty of men and women have wanted me, but I'd never lost my self-control with them, which was exactly what I kept allowing to happen with Kane. He was getting under my skin, and I didn't know what it was about him that affected me so much. I'd been in control of every aspect of my life all these years, and yet with him, I seemed to give way so freely. Perhaps it was the whole 'protector' thing he had going on, which was something I needed right now. I was just so afraid–I'd let it overpower me. I felt lost. Powerless.

It needed to stop, and I needed to be in better control of my emotions. It meant not doing things based on impulse or desire for Kane. I'd forgotten my-self into all this. I'd forgotten who I was and what I was capable of. I was a strong, independent and intelligent woman, who knew what she wanted and when she wanted it. I needed to remember that. I was and always would be a survivor. I'd given up too much of myself to fear, and it was weakening me. Don't get me wrong, I was grateful for Kane and his assistance. He was a man with a very useful skill-set, given these outrageous circumstances, but I needed to start acting like my own hero, too. At the end of the day, no matter what happened or how this ended, I would not let this define me. I would survive.

Chapter 12

Kane

I entered the bar with Kendall in tow, quickly scanning the area. There were at least two dozen people in there, and they consisted mostly of middle-aged men and women enjoying a casual drink. I'd have to keep an eye on them to make sure no one raised any red flags, but overall, this many people were manageable. I spotted Jeremy sitting at a table in the back of the bar, watching us with his brows raised as we approached. I'd neglected to tell him Kendall would be accompanying me. "Hello, Jeremy," I said as we sat down across from him.

"Well, I must say this is a pleasant surprise. I wasn't expecting anyone other than Kane, and frankly, my dear, you're much nicer to look at," Jeremy laughed, reaching his hand out to take Kendall's. "I'm Jeremy."

"Hi, I'm Kendall. It's nice to meet you," she replied, shooting him a flirtatious smile as she gently shook his hand. It was an innocent exchange, and yet it left me feeling inexplicably irritated.

"So…" Jeremy hesitated, glancing from Kendall back to me. He seemed uncertain about whether he should start talking.

"What did you find out?" I asked, prompting him. "You can speak freely in front of Kendall."

"All right," he said, taking a deep breath. "The rumblings are that something is going on with your brother. No one has heard from him for a few days. Not since some party he attended the other night, but apparently, he's been in contact with his staff. They've been managing business as usual. They were told he went on a last minute trip, but he didn't specify the location. He's been emailing them regularly."

I suspected someone had been emailing them on James' behalf, so as to not raise even more questions about his whereabouts.

The waitress came by, interrupting us. "Drinks?" She beamed, her black blouse unbuttoned far enough to reveal some generous cleavage.

"I'm going to grab a beer," Jeremy stated, glancing at us both. "Is that all right with you?" I nodded in response. "How about you, Kendall? What would you like?"

"A beer sounds great," she replied, casting him a warm smile.

"Beer...Really? My wife would never drink beer," he stated, sounding surprised, although I knew him well enough to know he was actually flirting with her.

"I bet she just hasn't found one she likes," Kendall answered tactfully.

"Do you have a preference?" he asked as the waitress stood, casting impatient looks at Kendall as she waited for our order.

"Not really. I'm open. You decide," she offered, flashing him another broad smile. Jeremy turned his attention back to the waitress to order our beers, and I found myself watching Kendall carefully. I was wondering what she was thinking about. This woman was possibly the most complex person I'd ever met, and I was beyond curious to learn more about her. She appeared to be studying Jeremy, and even I couldn't put my finger on it, but she seemed different somehow–her entire demeanor had changed. I found my thoughts drifting back to the kiss we'd shared at the hotel. I wasn't sure how I felt about it all, but she appeared to have put it behind her.

"We should probably wait until she comes back with our drinks to talk again," Jeremy suggested as the waitress headed back to the bar. He turned his attention to Kendall. "So, I know you drink beer, but what else is there to know about you, Kendall?"

"Let's see... I'm twenty-six; I'm a Capricorn; I like long walks on the beach. I just graduated top of my class with a master's degree in Business. I'm planning on opening my own online clothing store. What else…" She tapped her finger thoughtfully against her chin.

"You have a master's?" I questioned, feeling a little silly because I didn't know that. I remembered her mentioning something about graduating from school, but I actually knew very little about her. In my defense, I'd technically only known her for three days, but somehow that timeframe seemed irrelevant given everything that had happened between us since then. Not to mention that I'd been an asshole who had called her names, belittled her, and judged her, all the while not once actually trying to get to know her. I'd put in so little effort, and yet she'd managed to figure out a lot about me without actually have me telling her anything. Fuck, I am an asshole.

"Yes I do," she answered, sounding a little irritated. I couldn't blame her.

"Beauty and brains, I see. Have we met before?" Jeremy asked, drawing her attention back to him. "There's something very familiar about you."

"No, I don't think so, but I've been told I have one of those faces," she offered agreeably. "What about you? You said you were married. Kids too?" she asked, successfully changing the subject as the waitress made her way back to the table.

"Yeah, I'm married with twins, a boy and a girl. They're the best things to ever happen to me," he offered, getting the standard 'aw' response from Kendall. Jeremy did love his kids more than anything, and he was a great dad, although admittedly I was getting a little annoyed with the 'chit-chat'. I didn't bring her along to make idle conversation.

"What does your wife do? Is she a civilian or is she in the service as well?" Kendall asked, drawing curious looks from both of us.

"She's a Military Professor at the Naval Academy."

"Is that where you met?"

"Yeah, in our second year; it seems like a lifetime ago now," Jeremy replied. "But how did you know I was in the service? I never said I was," he asked, and looked at me as though I'd divulged something to her. I shrugged in response, because I didn't have a clue how she knew things like she did.

"Really? You're surprised I know you're military? Why? Because of your warm smile, blue jeans and a casual shirt?" she teased, laughing. "I've lived in D.C long enough to recognize you servicemen. Besides, you have military written all over you."

"I do? I thought I was fantastic at blending in with civilians," Jeremy grinned.

"You're all right," she laughed playfully, "but you still show some signs."

"What kind of signs?"

"It's hard to explain. Most people wouldn't even notice them, but I can tell you're still an active, uniform-wearing kind of serviceman. You're probably of a fairly high rank too," she said, pouring herself a glass of beer from the pitcher. "Plus you're friends with Kane, and although he hasn't confirmed his affiliation or the nature of his job, I have my suspicions. He seems to trust you, so you must go way back – likely to early adulthood. I say that because although you've lost most of your Southern drawl, it's still there and that gentlemanly charm was clearly born and bred in the South."

"Who is this girl and where did you find her?" Jeremy asked, sounding incredibly impressed.

"First, you tell me what you found out," I requested, hoping to get back on track, especially given that time was of the essence here. Besides, I didn't really like him paying this much attention to Kendall, or worse yet, them paying this much attention to each other.

"Right, well, your brother has made an enemy out of Senator MacFarland. It would appear that James was doing what he does best and was using his influence to block support for Senator MacFarland's pharmaceutical project. David Richton and Kyle Giles are said to have been overheard saying to Senator MacFarland that the situation was being 'handled' and that Senator Clarke 'wouldn't be an issue for much longer'. They also said Senator Clarke had enough skeletons in his own closet to play with, if required." Jeremy paused, taking a long sip of his beer before he continued. "Now, I tried to find out more about what kind of project your brother was blocking, but I couldn't discover much. I mean I could have found out more," he assured me with a cocky grin, "but not without raising flags. I do know that the project is associated with a product that is apparently revolutionary and will make them more money than anything else on the market. Whatever's going on, it's fair to say that your brother has pissed off quite a few people."

"Who are Kyle Giles and David Richton?" I asked, knowing the names, but unable to place them.

"Kyle Giles is a known lobbyist, who works for Markin Pharmaceutical Incorporated, and David Richton is a partner at one of the top law firms: Nelson, Richton and Associates, whom I assume represents Markin Pharmaceutical. Markin is a newer company, but it has quickly become the leading pharmaceutical company for mental health medication and supplies. Given the increasing volume of mental health diagnoses these days, the company is only going to get bigger," Kendall answered, further amazing me by how knowledgeable she was. "If he's involved and it's this big, my guess is its some sort of new product for a common condition they can easily label and misdiagnose. Probably a product for depression, anxiety or even addiction."

"There's one more thing you should know. They found Dominique's body. She's dead. It's looking like it was a homicide," Jeremy said. He glanced from Kendall to me. "Judging from your lack of reaction, you already knew that. With the rumors regarding the 'accidental' deaths of those three women, along with the fact that they apparently worked for Dominique... it would appear that shit is getting pretty messed up."

I nodded, confirming his suspicions.

"Jesus, what on Earth have you gotten yourself into?" Jeremy questioned, taking another long sip of his beer.

"Not me—James. He's the culprit here, and you're right, it's not good. I won't tell you more than you need to know, but thank you for your help, Jeremy. I'm sorry I had to ask you, but I was stuck," I stated apologetically, knowing full well that every time I involved someone in this mess, it put them at risk. Thanks to Jeremy, we now had some additional details to consider and I was almost certain we had a few initials we could match up to those on James' documents.

"You heading home tonight?" I asked, trying to lighten the mood.

"Nah, I'm going to stay in the city I think. Besides, it's nice to have a break now and then."

"I'll take your word for it. A wife and kids are not present on my long list of experiences," I laughed, unable to imagine how challenging it would be to have a family. It didn't help that I knew how controlling and difficult Sheryl could be at times, which had been causing strain in their relationship for years.

"What about your brother's girlfriend?" Jeremy asked curiously. "I saw her once at an event. She was incredibly sexy to say the least, and probably one of the most uniquely beautiful women I'd ever seen, although, Kendall, you might give her a run for her money. Word is that she worked for Dominique; her name was Raina or something. She's apparently the most sought after escort in the city. I guess she wasn't exactly his girlfriend, given she was paid to go out with him, but I heard they spent a lot of time together. I just can't wrap my head around why anyone would do that job. I can't see your brother dating a drug user or something, but who knows," Jeremy blathered.

I could feel the tension drifting off Kendall in waves at the mention of her former professional alter-ego. "Nah, she's not his girlfriend, but they are friends," I answered, clenching my jaw in frustration, "I've talked to her. She doesn't know much about all this, and she isn't a drug user," I said grumpily, trying to look anywhere but at Kendall.

"Sad that a girl like that would need to do something so degrading. Hopefully, she has some other guy taking care of her now," Jeremy continued, and I watched Kendall clenching her fists under the table. I didn't like what he was insinuating either. It made her seem pathetic and weak; granted I've had my issues with her profession but I now knew that she wasn't weak, not in the slightest. Hell, I'd been guilty of calling her down like that, too, but now that I knew better, it pissed me off to see just how judgmental people were. Their first instinct was to assume so little of her. I knew a part of her wanted to reveal herself and put Jeremy in his place. I knew this because I was currently fighting exactly the same urge, but we both knew better. It would serve no purpose to tell him she was Raina. If anything, it would only endanger her, and potentially him, too.

"Well to be fair, my guess is a girl like that doesn't necessarily need a man. She can probably take care of herself just fine," I offered, seeing a gracious smile conquer Kendall's lips.

"All right then," he stated, focusing his attention on the two of us. "How about you two? How did you meet?" he asked, motioning his index finger back and forth between us. "What's the deal here?

"We met at a bar," Kendall answered quickly, beating me to respond. "It's a rather boring tale of boy meets girl, but they remain just friends."

"Really? Just friends? I've never known Kane to be 'just friends' with a woman before," Jeremy pressed, and a small sly smile appeared on Kendall's lips.

"Yes, just friends... there are a lot of factors involved. I'm apparently not his type," she said, causing Jeremy's brow to furrow together in disbelief. "I know, I was disappointed as well, but he said something about not approving of some of my past actions. Having said that, you can imagine Kane wasn't the most gentlemanly of people when we first met either, so no harm no foul. No one is perfect."

Kendall leaned in towards Jeremy and cradled her chin with her right hand. "But the truth is, it's hard to find a guy who's a true gentleman these days. You know, a real charming man who offers his date respect and attention. I'd be so quick to offer my undivided attention to someone like that."

My anger spiked as I watched her whole demeanor change. I may have a somewhat more open-minded approach to her life choices, but this woman was unbelievable! In one breath, she'd presented false information, knowing full well I couldn't correct it and then she'd flirted with him for unknown reasons. It was shameless, because he's a friend who happened to be married. I could tell she was working him. I'd seen her in action at the party the other night, and truthfully, she was good at it. I mean, I doubted she had to try very hard to have men giving her attention, but Jeremy wasn't your typical, hard-edged, cocky military man. He's always been a real gentleman when it came to women, and she seemed to like stroking that part of his ego. It made sense now why James used her so much for events–she was good at this and could easily observe and adapt her behavior to people. By doing that, it put her one step ahead of them, which I imagined allowed her to retain control. I remembered my brother had always had a talent for this same thing, even as a kid. I could tell Kendall had learned a few tricks from him.

"I've learned that most women say that they want a 'nice guy,' but they don't. Trust me," Jeremy offered, sounding irritated. She'd clearly hit a nerve, which judging from her demeanor was exactly what she'd intended to do.

"No, that's not true. Women do love a good man; they just forget they do. Life has a way of catching up with us, and we can become critical and cynical in order to protect ourselves. It's survival. As a man, you just can't let them forget it. You have to remind them how it feels to be appreciated and wor-shipped. Men want this too; they just go about it differently. Relationships are so challenging because they get easier in some ways and harder in others. So much work is involved to not let things get complacent, but you get what you give in a relationship–at least, that's my motto."

"So are you exceptional, or does this apply to all women?" Jeremy asked with a flirtatious grin, clearly completely invested in the conversation.

"I happen to be exceptional," she teased causing a bubble of laughter to escape from his chest. "But no, it's not just me. You just have to give a woman what she wants, what she craves. Is it control? Affection? Attention? It all adds up to a kind of worship in the end. There's something about you that tells me you could anticipate a woman's needs quite easily. I bet you could give that special someone exactly what they want and need. I bet that lovely wife of yours would love to have this concept tested out on her."

It was such a bizarre and ass backwards way of working him. She had him practically eating from the palm of her hand, and yet she was sending him home to his wife. Judging from the wide, cocky grin plastered on his face, it had worked, too. I had to say, this little show of flirtation and manipulation was impressive, but it was also working my last ounce of patience with her.

"Yeah, maybe I should," Jeremy said, sounding determined. Abruptly getting up, he reached into his pocket, retrieving some cash and tossing it down on the table. "Kane, before I forget, I was thinking maybe you should call Damien Ryan and see what he might know."

"Damien Ryan? Oh right, he works for the Vice President, doesn't he?"

"Yeah, he's the Vice President's chief of staff. He's still going to be muzzled, but as a friend, maybe he can shed some light in the right places." Jeremy turned his attention to Kendall, who seemed a little distracted and gently grabbed her hand in his. "Kendall, it was a pleasure meeting you," he offered sweetly kissing the back of her hand.

"And you as well, Jeremy," she offered before he walked away, casting us one final salute before leaving the bar.

I glanced over at Kendall, who seemed anxious as she nursed the rest of her beer. My frustration with her far outweighed my curiosity about what she was upset about. Still, I didn't know how I could be so attracted to someone while being so angry with them. I mean, not even an hour after making out with me, she comes out here and flirts with a good friend of mine? What the fuck? This woman was driving me insane.

"We should head back to the room and check those initials," she stated flatly, breaking into my thoughts.

"Giving orders now, I see," I declared getting up and moving past her towards the exit.

After a few minutes of walking down the street, I heard her clear her throat. "Kane?"

"What?" I grunted, not looking back at her.

"I don't know if involving Damien Ryan in this is the best decision we could make," she said, stopping me dead in my tracks.

I slowly turned to face her. "And why not?"

"He and James have had… um… disagreements due to his behavior in the past. He's not a very nice man, and I don't think he'll help us. If anything, I think he will hurt us. I wouldn't be surprised if he was in on all this, to be honest. He hated James."

"And how would you know anything about Damien's character? Because of what my brother told you? Because of some little party you both attended?" I asked snidely. She tried to interject, but I wouldn't let her talk. I didn't want to hear it. "Yeah, that must be it. Well, let me tell you something. I've known Damien for fifteen years, and I'll make the judgment call on his character, okay?"

"Yes, of course. You just make the call with partial information and instead of getting the facts, you fill in the blanks with all your own fabricated information. You're good at that!" she spat, before storming past me, heading toward the hotel.

We entered the building and walked over to the elevator. She wouldn't look at me as we waited, and I was honestly flabbergasted that she had the nerve to try and tell me what to do. Tensions were high as we entered the cramped elevator space, and we both seemed to get angrier with every floor that passed.

As soon as the elevator doors swung open, I quickly headed down the hall to the room. She stayed in the doorway as I entered, and I automatically scanned the area for any signs of intrusion. Once I was satisfied it was safe, I motioned for her to come inside. I stared at her, and my insides continued to burn with an angry fire. I couldn't stay here with her right now. I needed to calm down before we got into an argument again, and I said something hurtful that I would regret. The bar was open. I could go down there for a bit and try to chill out.

"Don't leave the room. Don't answer the phone or the door. I'll be back," I announced, turning around to head out the door.

"Aren't you going to help me figure out who these initials belonged to? We're running out of time!" she stated, sounding outraged.

"No, I'm not. Besides you made it clear you know so much more about everything and everybody than I do, so have fun," I hissed, leaving the room and slamming the door behind me.

Chapter 13

Kendall

Even though Kane had been gone for over an hour, I was still baffled by his tantrum. He'd just stormed out of here like an angry two-year-old and honestly, I didn't know if he was coming back or not. I knew I'd pushed his buttons earlier, and it had pissed him off that his friend and I had flirted, but it was honestly harmless. I was simply trying to give his friend a chance to reignite some passion with his wife. I'd used this technique in the past with clients; at least, used it on the ones I could tell still loved their spouses and didn't really want to cheat. It was why I was so good at my job, because I was able to give them what they actually needed – not necessarily what they thought they wanted. So if I could help a client get revved up enough to go home and sleep with his spouse instead of me, so be it.

A part of me had been flirting to hurt Kane. I knew it wasn't the best decision, but I also knew he wanted me, so I figured a little incentive might push a man like him to make up his damn mind. I was wrong, and it seemed to have backfired. The truth was, he's a good man, but he liked to play it off like he isn't, and at that moment he had seemed incredibly lost. He's obviously a man who prides himself on not feeling any emotions, but I could tell he was battling with it. It was just incredibly hard, because he wouldn't let anyone in. He didn't know what he wanted and he was so fucking stubborn that he wouldn't listen to anyone, so I'd decided, right or wrong, he wasn't making the rules anymore when it came to the two of us –I was. I could very well be dead tomorrow, and honestly, I wanted him. I didn't want to have any regrets when it came to him. I didn't know why, but I couldn't shake the feeling that we were meant to have something together. Maybe I was being naïve, perhaps even delusional, but I could feel it in my gut. This whole thing with Kane was such a rollercoaster, and I was done waiting to see when it would stop. If he wasn't going to pursue it, I was. At least that way I'd know, once and for all.

However, I had to put all that on hold for a moment because I needed to try and figure out who these other initials belonged to. After an hour, I'd managed to link up some of the initials to senators, a few judges, lawyers and several lobbyists. Only a few of them remained hard to place, or unknown. It was easy to find the names, as all the offenses had taken place within the last two years, and once I'd identified the location of the offense, it was no problem to review other information like Advisory Committees and do some media scans. Most of the names belonged to members of James' party, including Senator Anthony MacFarland, along with his friends David Richton and Kyle Giles. That creep of a Senator Henry Kilman was among them, as were several other political representatives from both parties, but most notably Senator Elena Pine. James had often complained about her and how it seemed as though she was favored to run for Vice President alongside the current Vice President, who was running for President in the next election. Two sets of initials, H.S. and D.T.E.R. had a ton of very serious offenses like fraud and assault charges associated with them, but I couldn't figure out who they belonged to. I looked everywhere, but nothing was jumping out at me. It was probably because I was exhausted. Perhaps Kane would know.

I really hoped that Kane would let me talk to him about Damien Ryan. I had a bad feeling about him meeting with that sleazeball. Kane might think he knew him, but he really didn't. Damien Ryan hates both James and me, and would likely give anything to see either one of us suffer. He's a bad man – I knew this first hand, because if it hadn't been for James' intervention, I would have been sexually assaulted by Damien a few months ago. The worst part was, given Damien's position and my profession, even with all the bruises on my arms, neck and cheek, he would have likely gotten away with it. Damien had threatened James after he'd rescued me. He told him that if we didn't keep our mouths shut, he would make sure we would live to regret it. At the time, it seemed like the foolish ramblings of an angry man, but now... who knew? Everyone was suspect.

I needed a break from the documents, so I got up and walked over to grab a water bottle from the mini-fridge. I couldn't help noticing how nicely organized all Kane's stuff was. It was obvious he'd been in the military for a long time, there was so much control and precision in the way he kept everything; his clothes were neatly folded in his suitcase, his toiletries were immaculately arranged on the bathroom counter. Don't get me wrong, it's important to be organized to a certain extent, but life has a tendency to be messy. It can't stay controlled and organized forever. I learned that a long time ago; sometimes you just need to give in to the chaos.

I sat down on the couch. It was after midnight. I removed my bra, instantly feeling more relaxed. I laid my head down on the armchair, my eyelids growing heavy. I shut my eyes, and drifted into a light sleep. After what felt like mere seconds, I was awakened by the sound of the door slamming. I scrambled to my feet, panic-stricken that someone had found me, but instead I discovered Kane practically snarling as he stared at me.

"I had it all figured out..." he attested as he forcefully removed his jacket and tossed it on the floor. He was visibly intoxicated. "I was forced to take a leave of absence, so I figured I would come here and finally confront my brother. Tell him to stop trying to contact me. Tell him to fuck off, but then I saw him and then—" he stopped abruptly, taking a step towards me. I edged backwards cautiously. "Then I met you and it all went to hell. I didn't need any of this shit! I didn't need any of you. I didn't need people to think about and have to worry about. Hell, I was barely keeping myself together, and now I have to worry about you and James. *Fuck!*"

"You aren't the only one who didn't ask for this, Kane. I didn't ask for this either," I protested.

"You did ask for it! You asked for it, by associating with my brother. He's a disease. This is what he does, he hurts people."

"No, that's bullshit! You don't know him and even though I have no idea what any of this is about, James wouldn't be involved in it if it wasn't important," I stated, trying to control my rising temper. "I didn't ask for this! I didn't ask to meet you! I didn't ask to be involved in some fucking political scandal with people getting killed and corrupt politicians on the warpath! I was almost out of this whole scene, and now with each passing moment, we have more and more people closing in on us and we're running out of time!"

"Yeah, well you really looked like you wanted out of this whole scene tonight with Jeremy. You were working him pretty good for someone who wants out," he snarled, walking over to the mini-bar to retrieve a small vodka bottle and twist the cap off.

"What's wrong, Kane? Are you jealous?" I asked smugly, walking towards him. "Is that what all of this is about? Did it upset you?"

"Shut up! I can't help that it disgusts me to watch you acting like a whore. You keep preaching that you aren't one, but you could have fooled me," he spat. I knew he was deliberately trying to hurt me, but I didn't believe him. I didn't believe for a second that he was disgusted by me. He seemed jealous, so maybe my plan hadn't backfired as badly as I'd thought. At least he was giving me some insight into his feelings.

"Was I acting like a whore? Is that what a whore acts like?"

"Yes," he hissed through gritted teeth, taking a long gulp of vodka from the tiny bottle.

I stood in front of him, staring into his eyes. "Why do you say that? What did I say or do?"

"You were, you were—" He growled. "Why did you even do that? Flirt? I don't fucking get you!"

"What did I do that was so wrong? Complimented him on being a good man? Reminded him what it feels like to be a person beyond kids and responsibility? It was obvious his marriage is in trouble, and he's on the verge of cheating on his wife, even though he clearly loves her. It was also apparent that because he is a good man, once he does betray his marriage, he would never forgive himself for doing it. I just gave him inspiration to go home and fuck his wife to try to save his marriage, because it's what he really wants," I said, inching my way closer to him. "So that makes me a slut? That makes me a bad person?"

"Stop it!" he warned, taking a step back.

"Stop what?" I asked, taking a step forward.

"You're trying to manipulate me."

"No, I'm not. I'm explaining my actions to you. Was it my business to interfere? No, but I did him a favor, and he left that bar with a goal. I gave him a chance."

"Whatever, it doesn't matter. I don't fucking care about you and the things you do!"

"I don't believe that. In fact, I think you do care. I think you want me, and I think it scares the shit out of you."

"You have no idea what I want."

"No? Do you even know what you want?" I inquired, taking another step forward. He squared his shoulders defensively.

"It's not you."

"I don't believe that. If that were true you wouldn't be looking at me the way you have been, the way you are. You wouldn't be looking at my mouth and breasts the way you do. I think you should just let yourself want me," I said, now standing so close to him that I could feel the heat radiating from his body. He didn't move, but his breathing sped up. "You should let yourself go. Am I wrong? Tell me I'm wrong."

"You're wrong," he finally replied after a long, pregnant pause.

"Really? I think you're wrong, and you're afraid to act. There's not always a right and wrong, Kane. Sometimes in life you just need to make a choice and deal with it. Sometimes in life we get hurt and we stumble, but it's all about the experience and the adventure. For all my faults, I'm not afraid to take risks and put myself out there. I'm not afraid to take what I want when I can, and I'm not afraid to get hurt if that's what needs to happen. If you can't live your life that way, then that's on you, not me. I will respect what you want, though," I stated, not believing him for a second, but knowing I couldn't force him to take risks. I couldn't force him to be brave and vulnerable in hopes of achieving something great. I didn't know what tomorrow would bring, but I'd always been more afraid of risks I didn't take than the ones that I did.

"Kendall," he whispered. I could see the intensity in his eyes as he battled his inner turmoil.

"What, Kane?" I breathed, doing my best to stand my ground as he made up his mind.

With what seemed like lightning speed his lips came crashing down onto mine. I wrapped my arms around his neck, pulling him as close as he could get. As his kiss deepened, it felt like our bodies were fusing together. We stumbled backwards until my spine was pressed up against the cool surface of the wall. His strong hands ran down my back and onto my ass, as his pelvis pressed into mine, causing my sex to pulsate from the pressure of his erection.

My breathing quickened as he trailed kisses down my neck and collarbone while his hands slowly trailed up my pelvic bone and stomach until they reached my breasts. I lifted my arms, willing him to remove my top, which suddenly felt excruciatingly tight. He smiled against my lips as he hooked the bottom of it and pulled it up over my head. I shivered as the cool air hit my exposed breasts. His rough hands began exploring my bare chest; he licked his lips, which were hovering just above mine. I ran my hands up under his shirt and gripped his muscular shoulders. "Take off your shirt," I requested, biting my bottom lip as I tried my best to stifle the moan that was building in the back of my throat.

He quickly obliged, removing his shirt over his head and tossing it to the floor. He wrapped his arms around me and my nipples hardened as our bare chests pressed against one another. Our lips touched and a passionate frenzy consumed us both; my sex throbbed with need – I was desperate for him to touch me. I quickly unbuttoned my jeans, practically frantic to get them off.

He bent down low, gently tugging my jeans down to my ankles. I immediately kicked my way out of them. He stood up, running his hand up my left calf, up to my inner thigh, settling between my legs. He cupped my sex, gently applying pressure to my clit through my cotton underwear. I moaned, begging for his hands to alleviate the pounding within me.

"I've been fantasizing about making you moan for days now," he whispered, his lips touching mine as he circled my clit, continually applying more and more pressure. "The thought of you coming undone in my hands has been haunting my dreams."

"Then what are you waiting for?" I asked breathlessly, trying to stifle another moan as I ground my hips harder, complementing his every move.

"Whenever you're ready, baby," he said kissing along my jawline. My first orgasm released, sending a wave of pleasure ripping through every muscle in my body.

"That was fast. I had no idea you were so backed-up, Kendall," he teased in my ear, placing kisses down my neck and collarbone.

"I can't help it. Some guy's been messing with my head for days, constantly revving me up just to shut me down," I said, reaching down to feel his hard cock pressing against his jeans.

"What an asshole," he said, his eyes locked on mine as I unlatched his belt buckle and slowly unbuttoned his jeans.

"You said it," I replied, kissing his chin as I forced his zipper down.

He picked me up and carried me over to the bed, gently placing me down on it. He ran his hands along my body, worshipping every inch of it as he pulled my underwear off. "You're so unbelievably beautiful, Kendall." I don't know why but I was suddenly filled with emotion. Usually, sex was just sex, but even if this moment was all we ever had together, I'd be okay with it. I'd survive it, but it didn't change the fact that I'd never felt this way about anyone before, and it was intense. He'd officially managed to seduce every inch of me, including my heart, and it terrified me.

"Kane… Tell me—" I began, but stopped abruptly, afraid of what I'd be opening myself up to.

"Tell you what?" he asked, his brown eyes attentive and focused on me as he cupped my face in his palms.

"Tell me… Tell me you want me," I requested, my heart beating madly against my chest. I wasn't sure why it was so important to hear it, but I needed it. So many men and women wanted me, in fact, my whole job was to ensure that they did, but for some reason I needed to hear it verbally from Kane. I needed to know that he wanted me; that he wanted *Kendall*.

"Kendall… I've never wanted anyone as much as I want you," he offered sincerely, his lips softly kissing mine. A single tear escaped my right eye, and he wiped it away with his thumb. "My tough girl has a soft side, I see."

"I have many sides," I teased as he kissed me again. I ran my hands over his muscular torso; he was the sexiest man I'd ever seen. I found myself mesmerized by the hundreds of scars that covered his skin. I reached into his jeans, massaging his hard erection, and a moan escaped his lips. "Take those off, Kane." He quickly tugged at his jeans and boxers, releasing his heavy rod. I reached down to touch myself, finding my sex wet and ready. I moaned loudly as his hand replaced mine, sliding his fingers deeply into me.

"I think you might be ready," he teased, still sliding his fingers in and out.

I was more than ready. "I hope you have protection."

He was off the bed instantly, retrieving a condom from his bag and quickly rolling it over himself. He lowered himself on top of me and paused for a long moment.

"Are you going to make me beg?" I demanded. "I'm not the begging kind, and right now I want you to fuck me, Kane." I gasped as he let out a primal growl, his hard cock pushing inside me. There was no gentleness in his lovemaking, and right then that was just fine with me. I moaned, grabbing his muscular ass firmly, loving how strong he felt. "Go harder, Kane, I need you to go harder," I requested, knowing he was holding back. He obliged, thrusting his cock harder and deeper into me.

"Yes, this feels so good! Don't stop! Don't stop!"

"God, Kendall, you feel so good," he groaned, still moving fast and hard. "Tell me when you're ready, I'll hold off until you're there."

"Now," I cried, feeling as though time was standing still when a spasm of pleasure convulsed through me, releasing me into a blissfully relaxed state.

I felt him drop beside me on the bed. I looked over at him – his eyes were shut tight as we both struggled to catch our breath. "That was… That was…" he said, trying to catch his breath.

"That was about time."

"I know, I'm such an idiot. To think that we could have been doing that for days now." He laughed, and I joined in, chuckling at his words.

"I know, right?" I replied, and he leaned into me, gently kissing my lips.

"Kane…"

"Uh huh," he answered, his eyes closed again.

"How long until you're ready for round two?"

"Give me five minutes, and I'm all yours," he requested, pulling my body against his, wrapping his arms around me. Within moments, I could feel his erection growing against my hip. "All right, maybe less than five," he announced with a smile.

Chapter 14

Kane

I could lie here with Kendall in my arms forever. This had to be one of the best sensations I'd ever experienced. Don't get me wrong, the sex had been beyond amazing, but it was in that moment when I realized I never wanted to let her go. She was so special; I was ashamed it took me so long to see it. I grew angry with myself for treating her so poorly. She'd deserved better, and if we made it out of all this madness alive, I would love to be with her permanently. I'd love to have the chance to treat her right. At this point, it seemed like a pipe dream, but for now I'd take what I could get.

"Kane, can I ask what happened? What happened to make you go on leave?" she asked quietly, running her fingers along my forearm. "You don't have to tell me, I know it must be personal, but it's obviously affected you deeply. I mean... you don't even sleep peacefully."

"What do you mean?" I questioned, confused. I'd actually been sleeping better since meeting her.

"Well... it's just... you cry out in your sleep a lot," she whispered, her gorgeous eyes staring up at me, "You seem to be having nightmares."

I sighed audibly, my body growing tense in an odd combination of embarrassment and discomfort. I did owe her some sort of explanation. "I didn't realize I did that. Granted, I haven't really slept in weeks. I usually get a few hours if I'm lucky, but since meeting you I've actually gotten more for some reason."

"Really?"

"Yeah. I guess I've been going through a hard time. I don't like to talk about it but... the things I've been through have affected me more than I care to admit."

"Listen, you don't owe me an explanation and I can see you're uncomfortable. You don't have to tell me, Kane."

"No, I do. You were right when you guessed I was a Navy SEAL. The incident that pushed me into taking leave happened a few months ago. I can't give you specific details, but the long and short of it is that we had to go into a village where dangerous weaponry was supposed to be hidden. I walked into a house and discovered three young children —they were child soldiers, all under the age of thirteen and pointing AK47s at me. I tried to reason with them, but they wouldn't drop their weapons, no matter what I did or said. One of my men came around to check on me and he must have spooked them, because the next thing I knew, they opened fire on us. I had no choice but to shoot back. I saved us both, and he got to go home to his wife and kids. But that doesn't make it any easier to live with," I said, watching a few tears travelling down her cheeks. "I killed children who were only guilty of doing what they were taught to do. Wars at their core are horrible, but killing innocent children is not something I'm programmed to cope with. I started unraveling, and my superiors forced me to go on leave. They said I needed some time to pull myself together. For some reason, which is still beyond my understanding, I sought out my brother. Which, I guess, ultimately led me to you and this moment."

She sat up, placing her palms on either side of my face. "Kane, listen to me. I know this doesn't make what happened any easier, but you're a good man. Sometimes I think you forget that fact."

"I've done horrible things," I said honestly, knowing that a part of me had to be a monster, to do the things I'd done and the things that I'd likely have to do in the future.

"I don't believe that. Doing horrible things doesn't necessarily make you a monster. Sometimes they are necessary evils. They weigh on us because they go against our nature, but don't fool yourself into forgetting there's good in you. If you do that, they win, and truthfully it would be a shame, Kane. You still deserve good things. I've seen it in you from the moment I first spotted you, and you've tested my resolve often, but I still see it," she insisted, pressing tender kisses on my lips and forehead. I don't know how, but some of the pain I carried in my chest eased a bit. It didn't go away, but that brief moment of relief was foreign and so seductive.

"Will you go back?" she asked, nestling into my armpit and wrapping her arms around my torso.

"I think so. They want me to."

"I bet they do, you've been doing this for a long time. You're probably on track for a higher-ranked position, right?" she asked with a knowing smile. I grinned – she was still trying to garner information about my work.

"Yeah, you were right about that. I'm a Senior Chief and the plan is to be promoted to Master Chief, if I can get my shit together."

"If they thought you were damaged goods, they would have asked you to leave, or reassigned you elsewhere. They want you back, which means they want to keep you. Master Chief Clarke, huh? It has a nice ring to it. I could see you being good at that," she said, tracing one of the long scars on my forearm with her finger before skipping to another scar on my chest.

"For a long time, my work was all I had."

"It must be lonely though, constantly going from place to place. Do you have anywhere you call home?"

"Nowhere really. To be honest, I liked never having to settle anywhere for too long. I liked never having a connection to any one place, but for the first time in a long time I'm sort of hoping that changes."

"I can understand that."

"What about you? Is this where you call home?" I asked, curious about what her plans were. I hadn't ever really wanted to know anyone's goals before now.

"Yeah, I think so. I won't go back to Minnesota, so I guess this is home now. I've never really thought about it. For the past few years, my focus has been mainly on getting school done. I guess if I make it out of this, I'll let you know," she offered with a sad smile.

"You will make it out of this. Things are going to work out."

"Yeah, I know," she said unconvincingly as she tenderly kissed my shoulder. She began tracing another one of my scars. "Someday you'll have to tell me about each one of these. I bet they're very good stories."

I smiled, "Yeah, some of them are better than others. What about you? Any scars you can tell me about?" I asked, running my hands down her gorgeous curves and not seeing anything marring her perfect skin.

"No, not really, I have a few, but mine are mostly on the inside," she admitted, causing my heart to stop for a moment. I knew all too well that just because you couldn't see the scar, it didn't mean it didn't hurt or run deep.

"Kendall…" I said, hesitating for a long moment. I wanted to know how she'd gotten into her former profession, but that meant having to hear about her relationship with my brother and others, and I wasn't exactly keen on that idea. I decided to man up and ask the question. "How did you get into this escort business? You're so beautiful and so bright, I just don't get it. I didn't get it with James, either."

She remained silent, her brow creased in deep thought as she stared up at the ceiling. I was just mentally kicking myself, wishing I hadn't asked, when she spoke. "It's a sob story like so many others out there. I grew up poor in a rundown house in a small town, just outside Minneapolis. Truthfully though, I might have had a bed and a roof over my head, but it never really seemed like home. I always felt as if I was a stranger in my own life. I don't think I've ever really had a home. My father went to jail for burglary and drugs when I was really little. My mother was an uneducated alcoholic, who abused and neglected me, and who let others into our home to do the same. When I was eighteen, I'd finally had enough of her low-life boyfriend sneaking into my room at night when he tried to rape me. I decided to take control, and I've never seen or heard from her since. I moved to Minneapolis, worked a few jobs and got a job as a waitress in a high-end place downtown. That's when I met James," she offered. She stopped speaking for a minute, no doubt aware of the tension in my body at the mention of his name.

"Look, I was happy as a waitress, but your brother invited me to go to DC with him for a week, and it seemed like a free vacation. I was young and stupid, though not generally in the habit of taking off with grown men I didn't know, but something about James told me that I could trust him, so I did it. He introduced me to Dominique and offered me the chance to change my life. He taught me how to think and how to read people. He taught me how to influence them and how to seduce them, but most of all, he taught me how to stay in control of situations. I made a name for myself, made some money, and I went back to school. Got my undergraduate and master's degrees, and once I had enough money to get out, I did. At least, I was trying to. The party the other night was supposed to be my last one. I figured it would be easy, because James and I are friends. When I say friends, I mean it. We haven't had a sexual relationship since the first week I met him. I liked being his date. I just had to go with him, talk to few people, have a few drinks and then we would leave."

"But you have actually had sex for money though? Didn't that bother you?" I asked quietly.

"Yeah, I guess so, but it's sort of a yes and no answer. I enjoy sex. I didn't have time for a boyfriend, so sometimes, with certain clients, I allowed it to progress to that point. I didn't have sex with everyone. Like I said before, it's all about reading what people need. Most people who came to me thinking they needed sex, were actually just looking for something else. It could be understanding, comfort or a connection of some kind. Your brother taught me how to know the difference. I know it's hard to believe, but the skills are transferable to other things, particularly in business. Those are the same skills that make him so good at what he does."

We both lapsed into silence for a few minutes. "What's he really like?" I asked, knowing she knew my brother much better than I did.

"James?" she asked. I nodded. "He's smart, funny, cunning, incredibly charismatic and kind. He's been more of a mentor and cheerleader for me than anything else. That's something I've never really had before, and it was nice. He's a good man, and much like you, he's made some bad choices."

I shifted uncomfortably at the comparison; James had done hurtful things to me, but at the same time, I didn't think I could look myself in the mirror and ignore all the things I'd done to others. Suddenly, I wasn't so sure I was in a position to be as judgmental as I'd thought. "You know, he talked about you," she offered cautiously, aware she was venturing into a sensitive area. "He never told me your name, but he mentioned having a brother he was proud of. He said you had always been the impetus that pushed him to do better, to be better. At the party, after you got so upset, he opened up a little. He holds tremendous guilt over the mistakes he made with you," she stated, and I could feel myself pulling away from her, but she held me, willing me to let her finish. "I'm not saying what he did was right, but he did what he thought was necessary. He wanted to be better for you; he wanted to make you proud. It's his biggest regret, but he loves you."

I nodded, understanding what she was trying to say. I didn't know if I could ever totally forgive James, but I was able to accept a little better why he'd done what he did. She placed comforting kisses against my shoulder.

"I'm sorry, Kendall. I'm sorry for being so cruel and judgmental of you. I'm not in a position to pass judgment on you, and frankly, my behavior is more about me than it ever was about you," I offered sincerely, hoping she would accept my apology. My issues with my brother were one thing, but she hadn't really done anything to me, other than meet me in a bar.

"It's okay. I'm used to people judging me, but I'm not accustomed to people apologizing for it. Thank you. I'm sorry for disappointing you. For not being the person you wanted me to be, I guess."

"Please don't apologize for that. You're amazing. Even though I don't deserve your forgiveness, I thank you for it."

"We're all human. If a person takes responsibility for his faults and changes for the better, who am I to not grant them forgiveness? It's the ones who stop trying to be better, to do better who don't deserve forgiveness."

"You're a far better person than I am, Kendall."

"No, I'm not. I'm just trying to do and be the best person I can. Like I said, you're a good man, Kane Clarke. I just think you've seen and felt too much bad lately, and you've forgotten about the good."

"I think I'm starting to remember it," I admitted, tenderly stroking my thumb across her cheekbone, watching an adorable blush settle on her cheeks. "All right, enough talk about us. It's time to focus on James. I think you should fill me in on what you've found out about the initials, because something tells me it's going to be a crazy day."

"Agreed," she replied sadly, but her eyes shone with determination. We would get out of this – or at least, give it our best try.

Chapter 15

Kendall

We stayed up for hours, talking about what I'd learned about who the initials belonged to. We eventually succumbed to sleep and spent the rest of the night in each other's arms, which was honestly one of the best experiences I've had in a long time. After a few hours, his cries woke me up again, but I didn't mind. I had a new level of understanding regarding the demons he was battling. It made so much more sense now; he'd done something horrible, and he couldn't forgive himself for it. Over the past few days, Kane had saved my life and offered me protection. I figured if I could provide him with a few hours of comfort and protection from those horrible nightmares – that's exactly what I would do. I whispered soothing words in his ear, gently running my fingers through his hair. Maybe in time these words would bleed into his waking life somehow, and he wouldn't be plagued by these nightmares every night. I prayed I would get the chance to test my theory.

When he'd settled again, I got up and went into the shower. I was elated when Kane joined me a few minutes later. We'd made love quite a few times since last night, but this time his lovemaking felt different. More intimate. There was a connection and a tenderness that hadn't been there before, and it was unlike anything I'd ever experienced. I actually cried as I released, which was something I thought only happened to those ridiculously sappy girls. It was truly one of those moments that was almost indescribable to someone who hadn't experienced it for themselves.

Once we were both dressed, I found myself staring at Kane and cursing my luck. Leave it to me, to be on the brink of starting my new life and potentially finding the man of my dreams, only to have a target on back from a bunch of unknown killers. Ironically, I probably wouldn't have seen Kane again beyond the party, had it not been for all this craziness.

Kane checked his beeping phone; he must have received a text message. "Shit! I never thought he would actually see me."

"What's wrong?" I asked putting down the coffee cup I'd been sipping from. A fresh wave of anxiety rushed through me. I had so much more to lose this morning.

"Nothing, it's just I reached out to Damien when I took off last night, and he just texted to say we can meet, but I have to be there in thirty minutes. It means I have to go now, while I still have a chance in hell of making it through security in time," Kane offered, rushing around and grabbing his things.

I stood up and hurried towards him, panic coursing through my veins. I'd forgotten about Kane's intention to meet with Damien. I needed him to understand that this man wasn't to be trusted, and he needed to be careful. "Listen, Kane… about Damien, I really think you need to be careful what you say. He had it in for James and me. Not me, exactly, but Raina."

"Don't worry, Kendall. I'll be careful, I promise. I'm sorry I don't have time to talk about it right now. I really have to go," he stated, closing the distance between us and wrapping his arms around me.

"For the record, I think it's a mistake to talk to him."

"We're up against a wall here, Kendall. James doesn't have much time, assuming he's still alive. I need to try something and Damien's all I've got to work with. I'll be careful," he offered, giving me a gentle kiss on the forehead. "Stay put until I get back. I'll text you if I have any news."

I wanted to protest one last time, but it was too late, he'd already disappeared out the door. I couldn't shake the bad feeling in my chest; I knew in my bones that this was a mistake. I needed to make sure we had some kind of backup plan if everything went south. Desperation sent me into a frenzy, as I began to work through the piles of files, taking pictures of each of the documents with my cell phone. I turned on the laptop and loaded all the pictures onto my hard drive. I opened the email program and attached all the photos to an outgoing email in a zip file. I did a number of web searches, ensuring that all the major media outlet's email addresses were included in who the email was to be delivered to. I drafted an explanation regarding the contents of the email, along with information about what had occurred, leaving out the part about me being an escort, of course. I explained what I suspected had happened and that if Kane, James and I went missing, we'd potentially be dead. I made sure to include my suspicions about Damien Ryan being involved. I didn't have any proof yet, but I knew in my gut he was part of this. I set the timer in my email extension so the email would be delivered at 7:00pm precisely. That way, if all was well, I could cancel it, and if anything happened to us, at least the world would know about it.

Kane

"Kane Clarke! My friend, it's been a long time," Damien approached me in the waiting room to his office.

"Yeah, it has for sure," I agreed, placing my hand into his extended one.

"Please, come into my office. We can chat a bit before my next meeting," he offered, gesturing to his open office doors. I nodded, following him in and sitting down in the chair adjacent to his.

"Not that I don't like seeing you, but I suspect there is a purpose behind this visit."

"Thanks for making time for me, but yeah, you're right. I'm wondering if you know where my brother might be."

Damien frowned, rubbing his index finger against his temple. "Your brother? No, why would I? In case you weren't aware, James and I aren't exactly the best of friends."

"Yeah, I'd heard there was an issue of some kind," I admitted.

"No offence, Kane, but your brother's a dick, who has a tendency to turn his back on his own kind. Plus, that asshole sucker-punched me a few months back," he stated, pushing back in his chair. I was curious as to why James would actually hit him; he was a lot of things and he could be an asshole in a lot of ways, but he wasn't the type to be violent. His preference had always been to create action by words. It must have been something pretty serious to have set him off.

"Well, I bet it was a weak punch if it came from James," I joked, trying to put Damien at ease. This incident had clearly bruised his ego and I was hoping to encourage him to open-up a bit more about it.

"It was more the reason he punched me that pissed me off, rather than the actual punch." Damien stated smugly, his blue eyes softening at bit.

"Must have been over a woman," I pressed. I couldn't think of any other reason that James would get hot under the collar.

"Huh. That's a generous term for her, I prefer 'whore' but then again, that's just me."

"Beg your pardon?" I forced a chuckle, even as my insides clenched; I didn't like where this conversation was headed.

"Oh, you know – his little whore of a girlfriend –Raina, or whatever her name is. Anyway, this Raina – who's a prostitute, like literally, a professional hooker – she thought I was being too 'handsy' one night when I tried to acquire her services. Things got a little rough, and your brother accused me of sexually assaulting her and then he sucker-punched me. I mean, how could you even sexually assault a woman who sells sex? So ridiculous," he mocked, folding his arms over his chest.

Kendall had tried to warn me, but I hadn't listened; now my blood pounded in my ears as anger coursed through my body. I'd never wanted to harm someone as much as I wanted to harm Damien Ryan. For a minute, I thought about all the ways in which I could do it; deciding that I would take my time with his torture.

It took me another minute to realize that Damien had stopped talking and was giving me an odd look.

"Yeah, my brother does have a tendency to overreact," I offered, trying to recover my composure.

He watched me, his eyes narrowed. "I didn't realize you and James were close again. I thought a dislike for him was one thing we had in common."

"I wouldn't say we're close, but I'm starting to learn more about him," I stated diplomatically. Suddenly I was really hoping that I would get the chance to know James better. One thing was for sure — Damien and I had absolutely nothing in common.

"So he's missing you say?" Damien questioned.

"Yeah, I think he is."

"Any ideas who would take him, or why?" he asked. He deliberately kept his voice uninterested, but he'd made a mistake – he'd let on that he knew James had been *taken*, even though all I'd said was that he was *missing*. I decided to shake him up a bit, to see what might happen.

"I'm not sure; I know he's had some issues with a few of his fellow politicians."

"Oh? What kind of issues?"

"I've heard that my brother was making some accusations about some individuals, doing things that were illegal. It's stuff that would piss anyone off. Does any of this ring any bells?"

"No, I'm afraid it doesn't. Have you managed to talk to that disgrace of a girlfriend of his? I'm thinking she might have some insight."

"No, I haven't. I don't know her, but I doubt she would be of any help," I said. This conversation needed to end soon; I didn't like him talking about Kendall.

"Oh, I don't know – those whores can surprise you. They're often exposed to a lot of information they shouldn't hear... besides, at the very least, you might get a taste of what your brother seemed to be so pussy-whipped over." He laughed, making my anger spike again. "You all right?" he asked, watching me curiously. "You seem a bit rattled."

I shook my head, taking a deep breath to regain my composure. "Nah, I'm good."

"Listen, I really hate to cut this short, but I should head over to my next appointment," he stated, scratching his forehead.

"Yeah, of course. Sorry to take up your time, but thank you again for meeting with me," I offered, gripping his extended hand firmly and wishing so badly that I could press down and hear each one of his bones breaking.

"You take care. And, hey, let me know if you talk to Raina, or get any more information on your brother. I'll do my best to help, and I'll make some discreet inquiries on my end, try to get to the bottom of who took him."

"Yes, thank you. I'd appreciate that," I replied through gritted teeth as he sat down, reaching for his phone. I quickly headed out of the office.

"All right, Mr. Ryan, I'll cancel all your meetings for the rest of the day," his assistant was saying over the phone as I strode past her desk on my way out.

I quickly grabbed my cell. **Kendall, get ready. Something has happened. Will explain when I get there.**

I flagged down the nearest taxi and headed back to the hotel. Kendall had been right all along; Damien was clearly involved, and I suspected he was on to me. My performance in his office had hardly been stellar, and I groaned inwardly, knowing I'd let my feelings for Kendall color my behavior. As a SEAL, I was supposed to have a better handle on things. *Shit.*

Kendall

Kane burst through the door in a mad panic. "Kendall!" he said once he saw me, wrapping his arms around my waist. "I'm so sorry I didn't listen to you about Damien. What he did to you… I can't even handle that he did something like that to you. Getting punched was the least of what he deserved."

Anger was pouring off him in waves. I'm glad he hadn't been around that day, because the torn dress, scraped cheek and bruises hadn't been a pretty sight. "It's okay, I'm sorry you had to find out someone you thought was a friend is really such a horrible person," I offered, hugging him tightly, enjoying the warmth of his embrace. "You said for me to get ready. What happened?"

He held me for a moment longer before kissing the top of my head. "Did you pack up your things?" he asked, and I nodded. "Good, we need to get out of here. I'm pretty sure you were right about Damien being involved."

"Where will we go? What about James?"

"I'm not sure what to do at this point, but I was thinking of going to a café where there's Wi-Fi. I can try to hack into Damien's computer and see if I can find some clues about where James might be. It's a long shot, but Damien was definitely suspicious of me, and he's searching for Raina. He was pretty determined that I let him know if I got in touch with her. So we need to gain some distance."

Hearing the uncertainty in his voice had me on edge. I didn't like Kane being this unsure. Throughout this whole nightmare, he'd always managed to know what to do. It seemed so out of character for him to be worried, but right now that's exactly what it looked like. I know it was probably naïve on my part, or maybe just wishful thinking, but I'd always assumed he would fix this situation. But for the first time since this all began, it was becoming evident that we most likely wouldn't be able to save James, or ourselves.

I grabbed my laptop off the coffee table and shoved it – along with all the file folders we'd found – into my backpack. At this point, I didn't know where we would end up, so the safest thing was to take everything with me. I quickly pulled on my boots and tossed my jacket over my shoulders, running to meet Kane at the door. I watched him place a handgun into a concealed gun holder under his jacket. "Kendall," he said, his face fierce with intensity, "I won't let anything happen to you. I will fight to the death to protect you."

I believed him, and it broke my heart to think that he might die trying to protect me. If he died for me, I'd never forgive myself. I'd actually debated leaving while he was gone, but I knew that ultimately, it wouldn't do any good. He was involved now, whether I wanted him to be or not, and leaving would be signing James' death warrant. Given Damien's attraction to me, if worst came to worst, I thought I might be able to use myself as leverage to save them.

I was following Kane down the hall when I suddenly stopped dead in my tracks. It had dawned on me who the last two sets of initials belonged to.

"What's wrong?" Kane asked.

"Do you know Damien's full name?"

"Yeah, it's Damien Thomas Edward Ryan. A long pretentious name to match his personality."

"I know who they belong to. It's so obvious! How did we miss it?"

"Kendall, what are you talking about? You've lost me."

"H.S. and D.T.E.R. – those initials belong to Henry Samuels and Damien Thomas Edward Ryan."

"Kendall—That would mean that—You're saying the Vice President is involved?" Kane clarified, looking as shocked as I felt.

"Yes. That's why Damien is *so* involved. He's cleaning up this mess. You can't have the future leader of the free world and his chief of staff sitting under a laundry list of felonies."

"Of course! I should have known that. Dammit! This is worse than I thought," Kane stated, grabbing my hand. "We need to go." He took off again and we made our way swiftly down the hall to the elevators. The doors opened, and I followed Kane inside. I watched as he squared his shoulders, and his calm demeanor returned. He faced me and pulled me to him, his lips consuming mine. This kiss was unlike all the others we'd shared to date. I melted into it, surprised by the forcefulness guiding his movements – yet at the same time– there was a desperation in his embrace that made it hard for me to pull away. He slowly drew back and scoped my hood up over my head. "Kendall, keep your head down. If I tell you to run, you run. Go somewhere public. Understood?"

I wanted to argue and tell him I wouldn't just leave him. I wanted him to know that I was willing to risk just as much for him as he was for me, but I didn't. I didn't want him to be distracted. I didn't want him to worry about me not listening, so I didn't respond to his request. "Kane, I should tell you, I did something while you were gone. I uploaded—"

"Kendall, I'm sorry, we don't have time. I'm not saying this to be a dick; I'm saying it because I trust you. I trust that whatever you did while I was gone, will be for the best. You've pretty much figured out everything we know, so whatever you did is fine, and I thank you. I just can't think of anything else right now. They'll be here any minute, I'm sure of it. They don't know you're with me yet, but once they do, well, let's just say all hell will break loose. Stay alert."

"Okay, Kane," I said as he firmly took my hand in his. I watched the expression change in his eyes, as his razor-sharp focus took over instinctually. The elevator doors opened to the main lobby, and we were abruptly bombarded by the noises and sounds of the busy area of the hotel. We exited the elevator, and he led me down a long hallway leading to a side exit. Kane held his hand up, bringing me to a stop as he opened the door and quickly scanned the outside of the building. "Okay, let's go."

We walked down a long back alleyway, which led to a busy street opening. "Where will we go?" I questioned.

"I need somewhere public, somewhere busy with Wi-Fi access," he offered as we walked, his attention focused sharply on everyone and everything around us.

"There's a shopping center close by."

"That's perfect. Lead the way."

We didn't get very far, because without warning, two black SUVs pulled up beside us. "*Run!*" Kane shouted as men swiftly exited the vehicles and came towards us. We ran further down the street to the nearest alleyway and Kane pulled me around the corner into it. At the end of the alley was a wire fence, separating us from another back alley. Kane clasped his hands together, and I stepped onto them, gripping the top of the fence to pull my body up over the top. Kane took a running leap at the fence and pulled himself up and over, and we quickly climbed down. Our pursuers were very close, mere seconds behind. We made a dash for the back door of a nearby building. We'd almost reached it when two police cars came barreling down the alley, blocking our access.

Four police officers exited the cars with their guns drawn . "Don't move!" one of them warned harshly.

"I guess you don't need to fight fair when you've got the cops in your pocket," Kane spat at the four men who'd come at us first, but they didn't rise to the bait, merely grinned in amusement at Kane's frustration…I glanced anxiously at Kane, who was scanning the area, searching for an exit strategy, but it wasn't long before the two black SUVs pulled up, and we were surrounded. I realized we wouldn't be getting out of this alive.

A man exited one of the SUVs and approached us; I recognized him as the guy named Marty, one of the men who'd been responsible for kidnapping James. "My goodness, Raina, your new look almost suits you," he announced, reaching out to touch a strand of my hair. "Although I must admit, I've always been fond of your long dark hair. I've heard it looks especially good against your bare back, in dim lighting."

He was leering as he stepped even closer, and I could smell the stale tobacco on his clothes. He was almost touching me when Kane grabbed his gun. As soon as he reached for the weapon, one of the officers tazed him, and Kane screamed in agony when his body dropped to the ground, his limbs writhing. Marty ignored Kane's distress, keeping his gaze on me. "Raina, what's your real name, honey? If nothing else, Dominique was really good at keeping her girls' identities a secret. If the others had been smarter and followed her rules like you did, they'd probably still be alive."

"Fuck you, Marty," I spat angrily. My gaze was focused on Kane, who'd stopped screaming and was being hauled to his feet by two of the cops.

"Oh, how sweet," Marty said, slapping me so hard across the face, I could taste blood in my mouth. "You remembered my name." He yanked my bag from my shoulder and unzipped it, digging through the contents until he located my wallet, "Kendall Daley," he read aloud, and my heart dropped to my stomach. I'd worked so hard to protect my identity over the years, and now I was completely exposed. "Is it weird that I still prefer the name Raina?" He chuckled drily. "Load them up," he ordered as men swarmed around us. I tried to fight them off, but they quickly overpowered me and bound my wrists with zip-ties. I was forced into the backseat of one of the SUVs, where they shoved a gag in my mouth and pulled a black bag over my head.

I strained my ears to hear what was happening to Kane, but I couldn't. I thought they must have put him into the other vehicle. I sat quietly, but the only sound I could hear was the pounding of my heartbeat in my ears. The SUV started up and pulled away with a screech of tires. After what felt like an eternity, we stopped again. I heard multiple people talking around me, and tried my best to stay calm. The vehicle door opened and I was yanked out; whoever it was who'd grabbed me shoved me down onto my knees on the hard ground. I whimpered as small, sharp rocks dug into my skin. I could hear the rustling of leaves in the breeze and what sounded like waves crashing into shore in the background. A few minutes later, someone grabbed my arm and yanked me back up onto my feet, and I stumbled as I was dragged along a hard uneven, rocky surface. We stopped momentarily, and I heard the beeping of buttons followed by the creaking of a heavy steel door opening.

"This way, Raina," a man whispered close to my ear. My skin crawled and I averted my head, but whoever had hold of my arm squeezed the skin painfully and pulled me forward.

The echoing of footsteps told me we had entered a large concrete space. I was stopped, and the black bag was pulled off my head. I immediately scanned our surroundings and saw that we were in an old vacant warehouse of some sort. The scent of saltwater drifted to my nostrils, suggesting we were in a shipyard. Relief flowed through me when I spotted Kane by my side. Blood poured from a split in his lip, and the bruising and swelling around his left eye told me they'd done a number on him during the drive to our new location. Kane didn't look at me, his gaze was focused on something in the distance. I turned my attention to what he was staring at, and saw James. My eyes stung with tears as I stared at James' lifeless body each of his limbs shackled with heavy chains. It looked as though he'd suffered a lot; almost his entire body seemed to be beaten and maimed in some way. There was so much blood.

Marty saw the direction of my gaze and smirked. "Don't worry, he's still alive – at least for now." He leaned in to wipe a stray tear from my cheek and I reared away, desperate to avoid him touching me.

Kane yanked at his bindings, trying to get at Marty, but he was no match for the men surrounding us. They walked us over to two chairs, which had been placed directly in front of James. Relief spread through my chest when I spotted James' chest moving–he really was breathing. He was still alive, but I'd never seen a man look so broken. He was almost unrecognizable. We were shoved down into the chairs and one of our kidnappers removed the gags from our mouths.

"Now, I'm going to ask the million-dollar question, in hopes that you'll stop screwing us around and bring this mess to an end already. I'm tired; you're tired, and frankly, this has gone on long enough. Not to mention the costs in-volved," Marty declared, his menacing brown eyes fixated on mine. He turned his attention to Kane. "Listen, I know what you do for a living and that you care about protecting this country from harm. So as a matter of national security, I'm going to need any information that you've come across in the past few days. Where are the documents, Mr. Clarke?"

"I don't know what you're talking about. I don't know what any of this is about," Kane stated, squaring his shoulders defiantly. "If I *did* have any idea of what you were talking about, and given that you know what I do for a living, I'm amused by your definition of national security."

Marty sighed, his greasy blond hair falling into his eyes. "Oh, look at the big, tough man. While your attitude is very noble, we do have ways of making you tell us. For now, I don't want to mess-up Raina's beautiful face, but James here," he said, "has been fucked up quite a bit already, so we can just keep going on him." Marty strolled over to James and slapped him hard across the face, bringing him back into consciousness.

"Kane… Ken—" he rasped, his eyes filled with fear. "I'm sorry, I didn't know she would do that. I'm so sorry," he lamented. I didn't have a clue who he meant when he referred to 'she' and I peeked at Kane, but he seemed as puzzled as I was.

"You look confused, Raina," Marty said. He walked back over to me and ran his index finger down the bruised cheek he'd hit earlier. I flinched and turned my head away, but there was no way to escape his touch while I was confined to this chair.

"It's simple really." I heard a familiar voice announce as footsteps echoed towards us. "It's nice to see you again so soon, Kane," Damien Ryan said, his face lighting up in a wide grin. "And Raina, it's *always* a pleasure to see you. I guess you didn't know the full extent of James' little operation? He glanced over at James for a second before returning his attention to us. "It seems he and Dominique had been gathering information on various individuals involved in government, using Dominique's whores to do it. It was actually quite an impressive little operation. From what I understand, the information they'd gathered would be incredibly damaging to certain individuals it if was to fall into the wrong hands."

"You mean, it would be damaging for people like yourself and the Vice President? You might as well speak freely considering the situation, Damien," Kane spat.

Damien nodded. "Yes, you're quite right; myself, Henry Samuels... and many others. This information would be damaging to us all, and it would be incredibly damaging to our party collectively. It would take years to rebuild from such a scandal which is simply not an option, I'm afraid. Luckily, we've covered all our bases, and the last of our problems are in this warehouse. Everyone else who was involved has been eliminated, so if you'll just concede defeat and give us what we want, we can call this a night."

"Go fuck yourself!" I sneered, surprising myself with a sudden burst of bravery. I wasn't sure if it was the threat of dying in the immediate future, or the simple fact that I loathed this man, but I'd be damned if I was going to give in to this asshole.

"Oh no, Raina, that's never fun. It's always better to do that with a partner, as you well know. In fact, it's funny," he laughed, sending a chill down my spine, "I only started paying attention to you because of James and his campaign to destroy my political party. For months, I imagined teaching him a lesson by hurting you–but now, I find myself genuinely attracted to you. Perhaps before this all ends I'll finally get that little wish of mine and fuck you. Call it a parting gift, if you will."

"I swear, Damien, if you touch one hair on her head I will fucking kill you!" Kane threatened as two of our captors struggled to hold him down on his chair.

"Oh, please! Who the fuck are you kidding, Kane? I mean, you're good, but you're not that good. You won't be getting out of here; none of you are. All three of you will be dead soon, and I won't regret a thing. If we're being honest though, I do have to say that you being here does complicate matters \. It will be a little bit harder to cover-up your death, given your profession. I'm not worried about it though; it's merely a minor kink in the plan." Marty approached Damien, handing him the folders he'd retrieved from my bag.

Damien's lips broke into a wide grin as he flipped through the pages. "My, my, my James, you've been rather naughty and quite busy, I must say. I didn't realize just how much information you'd collected on everyone. Those whores really knew their way around a bedroom, I see."

"They certainly knew their way around *yours*," James croaked, erupting in weak laughter. "There's a ton of stuff on you in there. You think you're actually getting out of this? You're a seriously messed up individual, Damien."

"Wow, that's harsh judgment, coming from a man who used to be a whore himself," Damien sneered.

James shook his head. "You're right; I have made my fair share of mistakes in my lifetime –but at least when it came to me, people always *knew* when they were getting fucked."

"Did they, James? Dominique clearly didn't. Mind you, if she hadn't gotten greedy and tried to sell this information to the highest bidder, no one would have even known about this yet. Sure, we suspected you were a traitor, but those poor, innocent whores died because of *you*. They didn't know you were screwing *them* – at least, not in a way that was familiar to them."

"Their blood is on your hands, not mine, asshole," James shouted, spitting blood. Damien calmly strolled across to James punching him the ribs. James screamed in pain.

Marty crouched down in front of me. "Where are the copies of these documents?"

"I don't know." My eyes were stinging from the tears building up in them, but I held back. The last thing I wanted was for him to have the satisfaction of seeing me cry.

"Come now, there's always a copy somewhere. Are they on your computer? Just be honest with me, and I won't hurt you," he offered sweetly. He tried to touch my face again, but I recoiled and turned away.

"I don't have any copies. We looked for copies, but there weren't any."

"You can't possibly expect me to believe that," Marty growled, grabbing my chin between his thumb and index finger. I tried to move away, but he tightened his grip.

"Believe what you want," I hissed. I didn't see his raised hand until it was too late. He hit me hard across the cheek, and my eye erupted with pain.

"Cut the shit!"

"There were no copies, you moron!" Kane yelled. "You have her computer! You know what hotel room I was in, and you've already checked James' computer system and his house! Where the hell do you think these documents are? We've been on the run for days now. There wasn't exactly time to stop and make copies you, fucking idiot!"

"You think you're so tough, huh? A real fucking military superstar, aren't you?" Marty sneered.

"Please. Who the hell do you think you're talking to, Martin?" Kane scoffed. "Matter of fact, if you were half the man you think you are, you'd come over here and let me show you *exactly* who you're talking to."

Marty turned and punched Kane in the face.

"Oh, stop the dramatics, Marty. Really, do try and calm down. Kane is a top operative with the SEAL's, and he'd kill you in a heartbeat, given the chance in a fair fight," Damien stated disapprovingly as he strolled back over to me.

"Raina? Or do you prefer Kendall? I think I'm going to call you Raina. I hope you don't mind, but I'm far more attached to that name. How did these documents come into your possession?" he asked, stroking my hair. I yanked away from him, fury burning in my chest. What the hell was with all the hair stroking? Was it the go-to move, for sadistic assholes?

"She didn't have them, James sent them to me," Kane lied, spitting blood. "If your assholes hadn't attacked us the other night, Kendall wouldn't have had anything to do with this. She has nothing to do with this!"

"Oh, you poor, innocent thing," Damien cooed, pushing my bangs out of my eyes. "Sadly, I can't spare you. You're too much of a liability now. I want you to know though, that it does pain me to have to do this, it truly does."

His phone rang, and he answered it quickly. "Hello? Calm down, Anthony, I have the documents, and it's being taken care of. It's almost, done… Tell the Vice President it's being handled, and I'll see you in a few hours. We'll find some new girls, and then we can celebrate," he said, smiling at me before he hung up. "Politicians are *so* needy. Never able to do their dirty work themselves, always crying and moaning and fretting, every step of the way. I guess I don't have to tell you how needy they can be."

"I was just paid to fuck them, not to be a little bitch at their beck and call. But I guess it's a long road for you to travel, to become POTUS's top bitch," I retorted. My words were probably insulting us both, but I loved the way his face contorted with anger. I was getting a rise out of him, and it was worth whatever he might do to me in return.

"Now that we have the papers, perhaps we should get this moving, sir. We can investigate the files on her computer before we wipe it. And we have her home address from her ID," Marty offered, "so we can check it out, make sure there's nothing else."

"I do have dinner plans…" Damien replied thoughtfully. "I'm almost ready, but there's still one thing I want to do. Bring one of those barrels over here and get some matches and fuel," Damien demanded, never taking his eyes off me. I watched one of the men drag a barrel towards us, placing it in front of me. I had no clue what Damien intended to do with it. "Grab their bags and put them in the barrel. Hold on to her laptop and ID, I think I'd like to keep them, as a souvenir."

Marty collected our backpacks and tossed them into the barrel, along with what I assumed were James' belongings. One of the other men handed Marty a gasoline can, and he poured some into the barrel. He lit a few matches and dropped them into the barrel, watching as a burst of flames appeared, creating a flickering orange glow. "Soon, everyone will forget you even existed, my dear Raina."

Damien handed the papers to Marty, who tossed them into the fire. "Now, Raina–as promised, here is your parting gift," Damien stated, pulling me up from my chair and dragging me across to a nearby table. I tried to fight him off, but with my wrists bound behind me, I had limited motion. He bent me over the table, his weight pinning me down. I fought to get him off, but I couldn't get enough traction to do anything useful. I was terrified to realize I was pretty much completely defenseless with only limited range to move from my hips down. "Before I kill you gentlemen, I want you to witness this. It will make for a glorious final memory before you die."

"Get off me!" I screamed at the top of my lungs. I heard him laughing, and then the sound of his belt being unbuckled. *Shit.*

Chapter 16

Kane

Every time Kendall cried out it seemed as if a thousand knives were piercing every part of my body. I'd witnessed other human beings doing horrible things to one another, but watching Damien do this to her was too much for me. I'd never experienced anger and frustration as strongly as I was currently. My heart was shattering into a million pieces. The mental and emotional helplessness were far worse than any physical torture. "Damien, I promise I will fucking kill you!" I yelled, but my voice was drowned out by her shrieks, begging for help.

I noticed the men behind me had turned their backs on this little scene; clearly they didn't agree with what was going on either, but they were all too fucking cowardly to stop it. Marty hadn't turned away; in fact, I would have bet the sick fuck was getting off on it. "You're such a sick bastard for letting this happen! How can you sit by and watch this?" I spat at him.

He stepped in front of me, pressing his gun against my temple. "Shhhh... you're missing the show."

"If you don't stop I'll simply have to cut them off!" he hissed, as she continued to struggle wildly kicking any part of him that she could as he tried to unbuckle pants.

If only I could disarm him. I could kill them all, I was sure of it, if I could just get my damn arms free. I watched James struggling against his chains, trying with all his might to free himself, blood-soaked tears streaming down his face.

If a man who'd endured as much as he had could still try to help Kendall, I would figure out a way.

A loud crack sounded in the warehouse, followed by a groan which drew my attention back to Kendall. She'd managed to head-butt Damien by throwing her head back towards him, and judging by the pouring blood – she'd surely broken his nose. She shot up off the table and kicked out wildly, managing to hit him in the groin and then in the face as he crumpled to the floor in agony.

"Grab her!" Marty yelled, and the three men who had been standing behind me took off. Marty was distracted, so I snatched the opportunity to swing my legs up through my bound hands, bringing them around to my front. By the time Marty noticed what I was doing, it was already too late. I tackled him to the ground, sending his gun flying across the floor. I regained my footing and kicked him in the face before making a dash for the gun and kicking it further away, out of his reach. Two guys ran at me, one of them successfully tackling me to the ground. Fortunately, with extensive training in all aspects of combat, I was good on the ground. I swung my legs around and kicked the standing man in the knees, and he fell backwards. He got up again, but I elbowed him as hard as I could in the jaw, knocking him out cold. Scrambling to my feet, I tried to get my balance, but the other guy jumped at me, punching relentlessly until I stumbled back and lost my footing again. When I fell, he dropped his weight on top of my chest, continuing to beat on me–and I couldn't move.

"Get the fuck off of him now!" Kendall screamed, pointing Marty's dropped gun at my assailant. He held up his hands, stumbling in his hurry to back off and I pulled myself up onto my feet, hurrying over to the unconscious man and snatching up his weapon.

"Give me the fucking keys to unlock James!" Kendall demanded. Her still-bound hands shook with adrenaline.

"We don't have them," Marty stated with a smug smile. He wiped at his bloodied forehead, the result of my kick to his head. He had a sizeable gash above his left eyebrow, and already his eye socket was swollen and angry.

"No? Then what good are you?" she asked, her eyes wild with hatred.

Marty stared at her for a couple of seconds, clearly contemplating the gravity of her threat. Slowly, he reached into his pants pocket and tossed the key onto the floor in front of her. "How many other men are out there?" Kendall demanded, but no one answered. "Now everyone wants to be fucking silent?" she hissed, approaching Marty, who held his ground. "How many men?" she demanded, but silence ensued. Marty started to scream in agony when Kendall shot him in the thigh. The doors opened, and three more men rushed in. With my hands still bound it was awkward to grip the gun, but I couldn't afford to delay; I squeezed the trigger and managed to shoot all three of them, one after the other.

"There's three less now. How many more?" I demanded of Marty, continuing Kendall's line of questioning. We had to know exactly what we were up against.

"Fuck off," Marty groaned.

I shot him in the other thigh.

"Three!" Marty shrieked rolling around in agony. He gripped his hands against the wounds in his legs, blood darkening his pants.

"Now that wasn't so hard," I sneered. Kendall ran over to James and started to unlock the chains binding him. I watched as he slumped to the ground. I caught movement from the corner of my eye. The guy who'd been punching the crap out of me earlier was, aiming a gun at Kendall.

Damien had gotten to his feet, tackling me to the ground and grabbing my weapon. "None of you assholes better move!" he shouted, waving the gun at us. Three more men hurried through the warehouse doors with their weapons drawn.

"Where the fuck have you been?" Damien demanded angrily.

"What? Having a hard time doing your own dirty work? You need them to do the job for you?" I goaded, hoping to buy some time. If there was one thing I knew about Damien, it was that he needed to have the last word.

"You and I both know that's not true, Kane," Damien scoffed, glancing at his watch, "I'm done with this. I'm done with you all. Time of death–7:07pm." He laughed, turning to point the gun at James.

"Did you say 7:07?" Kendall demanded. It seemed an odd question given our current circumstances.

"Yes," Damien answered. He rolled his eyes. "Why on earth would it matter?"

Kendall laughed hysterically, and we stared at her in confusion. "You're all fucked. In fact, there's no use killing us now, you'll only be making it worse for yourselves." I had no clue what she was talking about, but as it was buying us some more time, I decided to let her go along with whatever she was doing. James coughed loudly and spat out a mouthful of blood, drawing my attention to him. He revealed a gun he'd somehow managed to conceal from the scuffle under his thigh, careful to ensure only I could see it.

"Just fucking kill them already!" Marty shouted.

"I wouldn't if I was you. I sent copies of all those documents to every major news station in the country. Secret's out – it's over for all of you," Kendall stated happily, a broad smile on her lips.

"You're lying!" Damien scoffed, narrowing his eyes.

"Nope, afraid not. I took photos of every single document and uploaded them into an email, which I programmed to be sent out at exactly 7:00pm. The email tells all the major news broadcasters about everything. All the murders, all the felonies you assholes committed; and I even gave them your name, Damien, and said if any of us ended up dead, you had something to do with it. I don't know about you, but I think you might want to stop while you're ahead, given the stuff they've already got on you. Another murder charge would only make it worse."

"She's lying!" Marty screamed. "Kill them!"

"Am I?" Kendall asked. "I did it before we even left the hotel, while Kane was meeting with you, Damien. I knew we needed to have a back-up plan. A type of insurance policy, or a *parting gift*, if you will." She paused, tilting her head to one side. "I think that's your phone buzzing. You might want to answer."

Damien reached into his pocket, retrieving his phone. He scanned the screen and I watched as his face fall into a horrified grimace. "You bitch!" he shrieked, running toward Kendall with the gun pointed to her head. I snatched up the gun from under James' thigh and shot Damien in the shoulder.

Distracted by Damien, I didn't see Marty move but when I turned back, I was terrified when I saw Kendall diving in front of me. I heard a gunshot, and Kendall fell to the ground. Marty had a weapon still pointed directly at me. I didn't hesitate. I pulled the trigger, shooting the bastard in the head. I slumped onto the ground beside Kendall, desperate to help her. Blood poured from a bullet wound in her rib cage. She'd shielded me. She'd taken a bullet for me.

The three remaining men had their guns drawn. "Drop your weapons and call for help!" I shouted, as they hesitated unsure of what to do, "It's all over. You'll be facing bigger charges if you kill us all," I continued, pulling my shirt up over my head. They lowered their guns, and one of them pulled his cell phone out. I applied as much pressure as I could to the wound, but there was so much blood, and her breathing was growing ragged. She was in trouble.

"Why did you do that?" I asked, a steady stream of tears falling down my cheeks.

"I couldn't let them kill you." She coughed, and blood dribbled down the side of her lip.

"Don't talk! Please just be still," I begged. I needed to be strong for Kendall's sake, but I couldn't stop the pained cry that escaped my lips.

"You wouldn't have had the chance to redeem yourself, to prove to yourself that you really are a good man. To me, that's worth dying for." She offered me a weak smile, struggling to keep her eyes open. "Don't worry, it doesn't hurt."

I sobbed, louder and harder than I ever thought possible, intense pain tearing through my chest ripped. This couldn't be the last time I held her. This couldn't be the last time I talked to her. "Please hang on, Kendall. Please hang on. I need you. I'm in love with you, Kendall, and I need you to be okay."

"It's about time you finally realized it," she teased, coughing again between shallow breaths. I watched her eyes shut slowly, and I was overcome with fear.

"Kendall, please hold on," I pleaded again, but she lost consciousness, and my world shattered around me. "Kendall! Kendall! Please, Kendall, don't do this!"

I cried. "I do love you! Please…" I reached for her neck, desperate to locate a pulse. It was there, but weak. "Kendall, stay with me. Where the hell is that ambulance?" I shouted. "Kendall, I need you!"

Epilogue

Six Months Later...

"So what kind of deal are they working out for you?" I asked as the waitress walked away from the table, taking a sip of my newly refreshed coffee. James smiled, and the scars on his face deepened. I had asked him once, why he didn't get them removed by a good plastic surgeon. I couldn't imagine wanting a reminder of being tortured on my face, but James told me he wanted them there, to remind him of everything he'd lost. He wanted them to remind him of Dominique; he said it was the least he could do, all things considered.

"My lawyers were able to plead out the patronization charge with probation. My testimony against the others will be key, given they want to make an example of them all. With everything that went on, even with a lack evidence, the prostitution patronage charge will be minor."

"Why did you start collecting information on everyone? What made you decide to do it?" I asked out of curiosity. Truth was, I'd wanted to know the answer to this for a while now but in the six months since James' ordeal, he'd never seemed ready to discuss it. Recently though, he'd lost some of the haunted expression in his eyes, and his mood had seemed far less bleak, giving me the courage to bring up a subject I'd avoided for six months.

"Listen, I'm no saint. I've done my fair share of law breaking, but I've never blurred the lines in my role as a politician. Believe it or not, I went into politics to make a difference. I believed in the value and responsibility of this job, as the voice of the American citizens. Perhaps it's hypocritical, but I don't see patronage as a comparable offense to things like drug charges, assaults, bribery and fraud. Some might disagree, but in my opinion, consensual sex on my own time is my business. Don't get me wrong, I've influenced or encouraged certain decisions or laws to go my way, but I've never removed someone's free will to make their decisions. I've never crossed the line into corruption. When someone starts using their position to corrupt the system and take advantage of those who are vulnerable, it's something I can't stand by and allow to happen without doing something to stop it.

He stopped speaking for a minute, as though he needed to collect himself. "Those poor women…" he said, his voice breaking a little, "…may they rest in peace, told Dom about some things they'd heard–pillow talk with some of their clients–and I was disgusted. When it started, I didn't know how deep this would go, didn't realize how much I would uncover. I couldn't believe people who I thought were friends were capable of these things. At first, I wasn't as careful, and I made inquiries openly. But when Damien attacked Kendall, to get back at me, it was the final straw. I couldn't let his boss – an extremely corrupt man – potentially become the leader of this nation. Senator MacFarland did some digging around of his own and discovered the information about my past and used it to try to blackmail me. I thought I could handle it, so I was reckless and threatened him back, telling him he wasn't the only one who knew secrets and that my past was nothing, in comparison to what I'd discovered about him and his friends. Word spreads fast."

James paused, his expression thoughtful, and clasped his hands on the table. "The threats escalated and Dom got scared. She wanted me to dump the information we'd collected, but I hesitated; I wanted do it at the right time, releasing it so that it could be used for some good, no matter how difficult things had gotten. My hope was to force their resignations in intervals. I thought it was the best strategic option, a way of getting justice, but not ruin the entire party's reputation for years to come. But I waited too long and Dom got edgy and tried to sell the information back to them and now, they're all dead because of it. That's the thing which will haunt me for the rest of my life. The fact that I hesitated and didn't take their threats seriously enough."

"You were trying to be honorable. You couldn't have known it would turn out this way," I offered, reaching over and gently squeezing his shoulder. It wasn't a huge gesture, but I wanted him to know I was there to support him.

"Honorable or not, it doesn't change that a lot was lost through my choices."

"Yes, but not everything was lost, and some things were gained," I replied, referencing our newfound relationship. We'd grown closer in the last few months and I was grateful to have my brother back in my life.

"Yes, you're right. Look for the positives, as Dom would say." James smiled, pouring himself some more coffee.

"The book deal will be a nice addition to your portfolio. At least you don't have to write it from a jail cell," I joked, attempting to lighten the mood.

"True. Although I always figured I would end up in jail someday, anyway," James stated. I gave him a curious look in response, and he expanded on the thought. "I'd have taken the fall for Dom if it came down to it, or ruined my reputation trying," James offered, swallowing a forkful of his scrambled eggs.

I leaned back in my chair. "I have to tell you…I don't understand. Why? Why would you have done that for her? She manipulated you into becoming an escort, and I know she was scared, but she was trying to sell the information you'd gathered. She's part of the reason why this all happened."

"Is that what you think?" he asked, sounding stunned, and he dropped his fork down onto his plate. "You think Dominique manipulated me into being an escort? That's where you're wrong, Kane. Whether you believe it or not, she *saved* me. I know I had to sacrifice a lot because of the choices I made, but she gave me the option, and she saved me when I was incredibly lost. I tried to do the right thing, but I got her mixed up in my quest for truth, and she's dead because of it." He paused, his brown eyes filled with emotion. "I would have taken the blame for her because I loved her, and she loved me. I know you don't approve of the life we lived, but it doesn't change that she was the love of my life. I would have done anything for Dom, and I have to accept that she's gone, because of me."

Dominique was the love of his life? I thought of the love of my life, Kendall, and how I'd felt when she took a bullet for me. Suddenly, everything seemed clear. I barely knew my brother, and there were a lot of things about him that I didn't understand, but I had no right to judge him and the love he'd shared with Dominique. I had no right to judge her, because I hadn't known her.

That's what the love of my life had taught me. She'd taught me that I judge people too quickly, and I don't give them a chance because of it. I knew better now though – she'd taught me to be a better man. "I'm sorry, James, I wasn't thinking. I didn't realize…" I paused, trying to find the right words. "I didn't realize how important Dominique was to you. I didn't even consider the loss you've had to live with. I'm sorry. Kendall would be so mad at me, for being such a judgmental asshole."

"Yes, she would." He laughed, swiping a stray tear from his cheek. "Dominique was a lot like Kendall, you know. Too beautiful and smart for their own good, they worked for everything they had, and they never bowed down to anyone. Dominique was more of rebel and risk-taker though, but I loved that about her. I think that's part of the reason why I was so drawn to Kendall, I know it sounds ridiculous, but they both had an almost larger than life sort of appeal."

"I didn't know Dominique, but if Kendall was anything like her, she must have been an amazing woman, because Kendall is the best person I know." I smiled, watching a warm grin settle on James' lips as well.

"Agreed. Dom was that for me."

"Who was what, for you?" a soft, familiar voice asked. My entire body was instantly on alert, as though it had been awakened from a deep slumber. Kendall sat down in the chair beside me and smiled, her beautiful gray eyes intense, as if she could see all the way into my soul. I'd almost lost her, but I thanked my lucky stars every day, that she was still with me. I was the luckiest man in the world to have the most beautiful, intelligent, brave and strong woman I knew, still here with me after her near brush with death.

James cast her a warm smile and Kendall grinned back. I'd finally come to terms with the fact that they were, in fact, just friends. I'd been so foolish and stubborn before, not accepting the truth. They did have a rather unconventional story and friendship, but now it was a part of our story, something that connected us all. I was incredibly thankful to have them both in my life. They were my family.

"We were talking about Dominique," James explained.

Kendall's expression grew somber. "She was amazing. She's greatly missed."

"Yeah she is," James replied, watching as Kendall stole a sip of my coffee.

"So, James, it's good news about the probation, huh? And the book deal? You're going to be a busy man," Kendall continued.

"Yeah, it's a relief for sure."

"Thank you, for lying about my involvement in everything. I owe you, for telling them I was an old family friend you were helping and that I was targeted for no reason."

James shook his head. "No, you don't owe me anything; they *did* have the wrong girl. You had nothing to do with what was happening. Besides, you were technically retired, from the minute we stepped out of that party, so it served no purpose to mention the escort part." He laughed. "They had nothing to charge you with anyway, so I just told a little white lie to save you some hassle."

"Technically true, but thank you, nonetheless," Kendall said, giving his hand a gentle squeeze.

"And don't worry, I won't be using any real names in the book either," James offered, and both Kendall and I offered him a relieved smile in return. "You've both had enough excitement because of me."

"I can't argue with you there," I replied, watching Kendall steal a piece of toast from my plate.

"How are you doing, James?" she asked.

James shrugged, seeming confused by the question. "I'm fine."

"No, I'm serious. How are you, really? Are you doing okay?"

He smiled, picking up his fork. "I'm a survivor, Kendall, same as you are. Don't worry about me, I'll be okay." Silence followed as James scratched his chin, examining Kendall thoughtfully.

"What are you looking at?" She laughed uneasily, an adorable blush settling onto her cheeks.

"I've got to say…this short hair you've been rocking is really growing on me. It really suits you," James complimented, changing the topic completely. James, being an excellent politician, was always good at controlling the conversation when needed and clearly he wanted to shift the conversation away from himself.

"Thanks." She laughed self-consciously, running her fingers through her hair. "I've enjoyed having the short hair, and its helped to keep me incognito through all the aftermath of what happened, but I'll likely grow it out again soon even though and I'll miss it. I miss being a blonde, every so often too."

"Yeah, it was a stroke of genius to change it so drastically," I offered, shoving a piece of bacon in my mouth.

Kendall's mouth fell open in shock. "I knew it! You did think it was a good idea! You said it was stupid at the time!"

"I lied," I admitted, chuckling at the outrage in her expression.

"Kane, you are unbelievable!"

"I know," I offered cockily, and it was Kendall's turn to laugh.

"God, you two are so sweet, it's sickening. Don't you have a flight to paradise to catch, or something?" James asked, retrieving his buzzing cell phone from his pocket.

"Yeah, I just have a few things to finish up for the website launch at the end of the month, before our flight tonight. Then I'm off to have some fun in the sun in Barbados with a certain sexy SEAL, before he goes back on duty for a few weeks," Kendall said, casting me a smile. My heart started to race and my body buzzed with the promise she offered in that smile.

"I'm proud of you, Kendall. You've been through a lot, but you haven't let it stop you. You've worked hard, and you deserve this little pre-launch vacation," James stated. He stood up pulling some bills from his pocket, and tossing them on the table. "Listen, I do have to get going though, I have a meeting with a prospective new client."

"Client for what?" I asked in confusion.

"Oh, didn't you hear?" Kendall asked, her eyebrows arched with amusement. "James, our soon-to-be-writer, is also going to be working as a political consultant for aspiring politicians."

"You've got to be kidding me. I thought for sure you were done with politics, given everything that happened," I replied. I think my jaw had dropped, practically scraping the top of the table.

"Well, you thought wrong. I know politics better than anyone and I'm the new hot ticket in town. They all want my expertise, because the good politicians think I'm noble, and the bad politicians hate me – but think I have some tricks of the trade to share. So frankly, business is good either way," James laughed. He walked around the table, opening his arms to me for an embrace. "You two have fun in paradise, and be sure to take care of Kendall. Although something tells me she may take care of you, just as much, if not more."

"You bet I do," Kendall laughed, being pulled into James' arms for a tight hug. He waved one last time and walked away from the table.

"I can't wait to be on the beach with you, sipping on cocktails," I said as Kendall leaned into me, pressing a tender kiss to my lips that sent a wave of heat flashing through my body, melting me to the core as only she could.

"Me either, babe. I'll be the one rocking the bikini and the bullet scar," she joked, tapping the site of the now-healed wound. I pulled her onto my lap and wrapped my arms around her protectively. That scar would always be a reminder of the sacrifice she'd made to save my life. She'd almost been raped and died—I would never be able to forget that.

"You're still the most gorgeous woman to walk the face of the planet," I replied, kissing the tip of her nose and then her lips. "Listen, I was thinking you could also be rocking something else on the beach."

"What are you talking about, Kane?" she asked, her brows knitted together in suspicion. "I know you. You're up to something."

"I was thinking you could be rocking a ridiculously sexy bikini, along with a new rock on a certain special finger."

"What are you talking about?" she questioned, but I could see the twinkle of excitement which appeared in her gray eyes.

"I was going to wait until we got to Barbados, but considering I've been walking around with this thing in my wallet for months now… I think I'd rather see it on your finger and watch as the tropical sunlight hits it for the first time. And I'd love to have a few more days of hearing you calling me your fiancé, before I get shipped off to who-knows-where with a bunch of dudes." I helped her off my lap and knelt down on one knee in front of her, ignoring the other people in the restaurant as she stared and began to grin. "Kendall Daley, you are the most amazing woman I've ever had the privilege of knowing, let alone loving. Will you do me the great honor of being my partner, my better half in all ways, and make me the luckiest man in the world by agreeing to become my wife?"

"Are you sure about this?" she asked. Her matter-of-fact response sucked the romance out of the moment, but was so typically Kendall. She was cautious, and wanted complete honesty from me, as she'd demanded almost from the moment we met. "If we do this, it means that I'm letting you in completely. It means that I trust you completely, and I expect the same from you. If we do this, it means that I'm giving you my entire heart and soul."

I answered, ensuring that my sincerity was visible in every nuance of my expression. "I know, and I've never been more certain of anything in my life."

"I hope you know what you're getting yourself into," she laughed, launching herself into my arms. "Of course I will!" She was wiping tears away from her cheeks before her lips claimed mine and my whole body warmed with happiness. When she pulled back, she eyed me cautiously. "You know there are probably going to be a lot more difficult days, than happy ones," she stated seriously, her gaze intense. Those same eyes had always managed to see right through me. She could see things I didn't even know were there. I couldn't hide from her and for the first time in my life, I didn't want to.

"There will be, but nothing we can't handle. You've saved me in more ways than one, Kendall, and as long as I have you to remind me of the good in this life, the rough days won't last forever. So for the record – is that officially a yay or nay?"

"I love you, Kane. Definitely yay to it all," she smiled, entwining her fingers in mine. And in that moment, I knew that we both finally felt like we were home, for the first time in our lives.

About the Author

I'm an avid reader (and dreamer) who hails from northern Ontario Canada where I live with my husband and fur babies. I hope my stories provide you with an escape and some entertainment for a little while (that's really all I can ask for).

Find me and follow me on:

- Twitter: @JessicaPageAuth

- On Facebook:
  https://www.facebook.com/jessicapageauthor

- Feel free to visit my website:
  http://jessicapagenovels.wix.com/jessicapageauthor

- On Goodreads:
  https://www.goodreads.com/author/show/8395779.Jessica_Page